# After The Bell Rings

Sept. 12, 2009

Taylor,
Schoolhouse stories and unique illustrations brought this book together.
Enjoy,
LeAnne Brogan

# After The Bell Rings

## LeAnne Brogan

*Kids' stories and teachers' stories,
Presented by the lady in the library.*

Copyright © 2008 by LeAnne Brogan.

ISBN:        Softcover                978-1-4363-5019-8

All rights reserved. No part of this book may be reproduced or transmitted in any form or by any means, electronic or mechanical, including photocopying, recording, or by any information storage and retrieval system, without permission in writing from the copyright owner.

This is a work of fiction. Names, characters, places and incidents either are the product of the author's imagination or are used fictitiously, and any resemblance to any actual persons, living or dead, events, or locales is entirely coincidental.

This book was printed in the United States of America.

**To order additional copies of this book, contact:**
Xlibris Corporation
1-888-795-4274
www.Xlibris.com
Orders@Xlibris.com
49506

# Contents

Introduction ................................................................................. 11

Chapter 1: From a Kid's Point of View ........................................ 15
Chapter 2: Kindergarten shares their positive thoughts ............... 25
Chapter 3: Writers of First Grade relay what they
    would like to be when they grow up ..................................... 27
Chapter 4: Writers of Second Grade relay what makes them happy ............ 29
Chapter 5: Writers of Third Grade share their favorite book ....... 32
Chapter 6: Writers of Fourth Grade were asked:
    If you could name a new star or planet,
    what would you name it and why? ......................................... 35
Chapter 7: Writers of Fifth Grade were asked:
    If you could visit any place in the world,
    where would you visit and why? ............................................. 39
Chapter 8: Writers of Sixth Grade were asked this question:
    Name someone who has inspired you and why?
    It could be a member of your family, a friend, or other .......... 45
Chapter 9: Writers of Seventh Grade were asked—
    What or who is the most amazing person, time, place,
    or thing you have ever seen? .................................................... 52
Chapter 10: Writers of Eighth Grade share something
    that they love about their grandmother or grandfather .......... 59
Chapter 11: One-liners and Briefs ................................................ 64
Chapter 12: Acronyms ................................................................... 71
Chapter 13: Kids' Homework Excuses .......................................... 73
Chapter 14: Parents' Excuses: Calling their kids off from school .... 75

From a Teacher's Point of View ..................................................... 79

Dedicated to students, educators and parents

# Acknowledgements

I would like to thank the children that I work with every day of the school year at the Drums Elementary / Middle School, located in the Keystone State of Northeastern Pennsylvania. "Thanks kids," for enabling me to see firsthand your toothless grins, sometimes unending fears, the newest fashion trends and your rainy day tears. Thank you for introducing me to your parents, siblings, friends, and faithful pets, especially those who ran in the door after you! Tender appreciation to the kids who sprinkled their cheer in the breakfast room consuming their glazed honey cinnamon sugar donuts, super-sized cream cheese and pizza bagels, Apple Jacks and Lucky Charms cereal, ham and cheese English muffins, assorted juices and 2% white, chocolate, or strawberry milk.

You became energized by the bright-eyed cafeteria women who made sure you started your day with good nutrition. To the siblings that entered the school holding hands, and the siblings who tormented one another each morning in the hallway, you showed me a sign of sibling rivalry and kinship. And to the kindergarten kids who showed me their weekly "show and tell" items, (exclusively from A-Z), to birthday celebrators sharing your delightful home-made treats, for the Valentines, artwork, projects, gifts, good wishes, songs, waves, chants and cheers, you made my day, every day.

I would like to give a warm and special thank you to our very own Hazleton Area School District middle school art teacher, Lisa DeSpirito, for her superb sketches in the first chapter, "From a kid's point of view."

Also, I thank my cover design illustrator, the youthful and talented high school senior, Megan Zahay. You are a remarkable, outstanding, gifted, first-class, captivating young woman! A bright and promising future awaits you. I wish to compliment and recognize your gift.

Thank you to the teachers, faculty, staff members and the students of the Hazleton, Weatherly, North Pocono and MMI Area School Districts. They contributed short excerpts jogged from their memories to assist me in putting together, "From a Teachers Point of View" and the "Writers from Grades 1-Grade 8" with their short stories.

To all parents of every exceptional child, hats off to you!

# Introduction

My first publication, *Inside Amy, Adults and Eating Disorders—Out in the Open*, was a personal journey through acceptance and recovery from the eating disorder, anorexia nervosa. In my recovery process, with the support of my loving family, friends and my faith in God, I discovered my gift of writing. Writing enhances my expression. Pencil or pen to paper comes more naturally to me than voicing my feelings and emotions. Solitude gives me comfort and peace. It is my time to listen, reflect and write. I love to absorb my surroundings when I am outdoors. I have a special fondness for the sounds of nature. There is no question why I work in a library.

The expression and title *"After the Bell Rings,"* pertains to that special time when children leave their parents behind and walk proudly through the schoolhouse doors as mother, father, grandparent or guardian wishes and worries and wants to watch and wonders and feels woozy and worthy and worldly about what their children do in school every day. I've heard parents say, "If only I could be an itsy, bitsy teeny weenie fly on the wall." "I'd give anything to see what Emily and Marvin, and Casey and Candice do in school all day." Working in the Drums School, I consider myself that fly. *After the Bell Rings* will share numerous stories with all of you interested readers of events that have happened.

A child lies within each of us. Working with children in school every day, I see firsthand, as do their teachers, faculty and staff members, their individual traits, successes, weaknesses, and challenges. Each child, like myself (40 or so years ago, however, still young at heart) grows and matures from an "on-the-go toddler, tenacious teenager, into a hopefully assured and responsible adult. When we reach that wonderful age of 50, that's when wisdom kicks in. When you're a kid, you know everything. When you gain wisdom, you have everything. What will a child become when he or she grows up? Early dreams and visions of becoming an MLB baseball or NBA basketball player, a Hollywood actor or actress, state policeman, fireman, or nurse, often transform into different and opposite career decisions.

My childhood dreams were those of a highly paid fashion model, an Olympic gymnast, a TWA flight attendant, or a renowned interior designer. I became a production worker at a factory, (it was only for the money fresh out of high school) a dental assistant, a wife, a mother, a librarian, a writer and an author. Many different hats, wouldn't you agree? Hey kids, you can have many hats too and set goals and dreams to be anything you want to be. Only you can make it happen.

Inside this book, I guesstimate what several children might grow up to be, simply by being there after the bell rings. With the assistance of a group of invaluable teachers and co-workers, along with the students themselves, we have included and shared several whole-hearted, heartfelt and heart-happy stories. Happy reading!

From the listening, observing, watchful eye
Of the students who daily pass me by.
Hunter and Carley, Ryan and Kate,
Ready for school, dare not be late.

Sleepy or smiling
A few of them pout.
Most are enthusiastic
Until the day's almost out.

Month after month
We count down the days.
The homework and projects
The dreaded PSSA's.

All of a sudden
We're changing the clocks.
Field trips and recess,
Ah, the summer break rocks!

# Chapter 1

## From a Kid's Point of View

Why do some students, like Aaron, have to be the first in line? Because Aaron will become a first-line manager, a captain, a bigwig, a kingpin or an executive administrator. First is foremost. First is not always the best. Get it right the first time. Ladies first! You are first rate.

Why do some kids like Megan insist on being the last student in line, shuffling their way around the other kids, procrastinating, pushing and shoving for last place? Because Megan will become an advocate, an admirer, a life insurance agent, a supporter for women's rights, or perhaps a funeral director. Last is conclusive. Last is most recent. Last is final. Last is a thing of the past. Last one's a rotten egg! Last or first, no better, no worse.

*I want to be a doctor.*

Why does Brandon jump up and down, dance and turn around, clinch his legs tightly together and asks politely and affirmatively in a high-pitched voice, "I have to go pee, or potty," or "Kin I go to the baff room?" Because Brandon has expression and can speak for himself, he will become valedictorian of his graduating class, a prominent television broadcaster, a government chief executive legislator, a politician, lawyer, or perhaps a preacher.

Remember, use your words; your voice matters.

Why do Rachel, Christian, Steven, Samantha, Angel and Dylan ask so many questions? These kids are eager for information, inquisitive and extremely anxious to mature. "SLOW DOWN," there is plenty of time until you become a doctor of psychiatry, psychology, an architectural engineer, a computer technologist, a motion picture director, a taxi driver, chauffeur, or a veterinarian.

Ask and receive; seek and find. The more questions you ask, guarantees you will always be on task.

Wishes and dreams can come true. Believe it.

Why do some girls like Michele, Heather, and Casey giggle and giggle and giggle? Is it possible that a seven-year-old's growth spurt triggers this behavior? Do they ingest some foreign mysterious ingredient from flavored lip glosses? Do their funny bones inadvertently spread to their senses? Ah, must be the saying, "Girls will be girls." Call them Happy Campers, Timely Trios, Flushed Feminists, Feverish Females, Modest Maidens, Lighthearted Ladies, and Warmhearted, Well-off-Women. I see them frolicking in designer dress shops and sitting at the counters of make-up artists. I also see them as Mindful Mothers tending to their Cherished Children.

*I want to be a lawyer.*

Laughter is the best medicine for your heart, and it also adds spice to your life!

Why did Mary Rose come to school every day wearing on her head a beautifully color-coordinated bandana, which complimented her flawless outfit? Mary Rose was in remission from leukemia and had lost her hair. Some days she appeared a bit sallow and sad. On good days, she was friendly and happy and content. I prayed for Mary Rose every time I saw her. A miracle could happen. She will become a physical therapist or a nurturing caregiver in a health related profession. Say a prayer for all the Mary Roses in the world. Some special children are needed in special places as very special angels.

In the cafeteria lunch line, why do Joey, Justin and Evan bump, push, pinch, poke, flick, tug and tickle one another every single day?

"It was just an accident," Joey responded.

"Wasn't me," Justin whined.

"I didn't mean to," Evan pleaded.

They remind me of the Three Stooges, "Oh a wise guy, huh?" "Why soitenly!" "What's the idea?" "Keep your hands to yourself!" I tell them.

Kids need their lunch period to unwind. They have been as motionless as tuxedoed penguins all morning long in their classrooms. Dressed for dinner, they are now given the opportunity to move more freely, still adhering to the cafeteria rules, and they are hungry! Imagine releasing two hundred thirteen penguins, seated by classrooms and gathering the troops into a lunch line.

*I want to be a First Grade teacher.*

This trio of boys could join the circus and become classic clowns, could be considered as game show hosts, or our future comedians. A suggestion to all kids in the cafeteria: fuel up, recharge your kid batteries, and give your teachers the best you've got for the afternoon. And, have a good healthy lunch! Maybe, just maybe, if you do your best, your appreciative teachers will put in *Happy Feet* on DVD after lunch.

Why do boys have to make those funky fart sounds by cupping their right hand underneath their left armpit, and with quick, rapid jerking motions, bodacious fart sounds abound? As they laugh hysterically out loud to tears, they continue the gestures. I've even witnessed kids cupping their hand behind their knee, bending the knee swiftly and ever so aggressively. Sounds emit creating more laughter than the armpit sounds! Not every kid has this special talent. It does take practice. A group of kids engaging in this activity looks like the fans jammin' at a rock concert or a very abnormal EKG. I'll admit, no matter how hard I try to, I can't make those sounds. Guess it's for "KIDS" only. With that amount of agility and coordination, I see a future Harlem Globetrotter, World Championship gymnast or an acrobat in the Ringling Brothers Barnum & Bailey Circus.

While we're on the subject, just imagine what goes down in the classroom when a kid farts! The odor is noticed immediately, as quickly as you recognize the scent of a passing skunk surging through your nostrils. A red alert! A fast hand covers the mouth and nose. The "EEEUUU" grimace contorts the facial features.

"Somebody farted, flurped, broke wind, or passed gas."

"Who stepped on a duck?"

"Who cut the cheese?" Everyone looks around for the probable suspect. Fingers are pointed and accusations are thrown.

*I want to be a substitute teacher.*

"Whoever smelt it, dealt it."
"Whoever denied it, supplied it," the kids roar.
"It smells like a rotten egg. It smells like a hundred rotten eggs!"
"What did you eat?"
Gratefully, gloriously, and gleefully, the stench dissipates, the atmosphere slowly becomes unpolluted, and the kids can breathe freely once more. This kid (the subject) enjoys fine cuisine. I predict he'll have his very own cooking show on Cable-TV. On the count of three, inhale deeply, expanding your belly, hold that breath for three seconds, now exhale slowly through your mouth. The episode has ended. Next time, get the tropical rainforest air freshener ready!

Patty, an imaginative kindergarten student, ingeniously traded part of her lunch with gullible Grace in the cafeteria. She said to Judy, the lunch lady, holding and wagging a baggie with carrot and celery sticks inside it, "I can't eat these vegetables." "They give me a rash." She proudly traded her veggies for three gooey chocolaty peanut butter chunks of Gracie's mom's homemade fudge. "These will make me sweeter and HYPER," she said.

Patty is persuasive. Persuasion will make her a fine defensive lawyer one day. Like any other edible tidbit, fudge is truly a sugary delight, eaten in moderation, of course. Go ahead, indulge! Isn't it all fat and calorie free?

Why do kids get such a zing out of saying *wiener*, rather than *hot dog*? Twins Cody and Carson played a game of catch in their backyard one blazing summer afternoon, as a young girl walked by with her dachshund, Delilah. "Weiner dog, wiener dog!" the boys shouted and pointed and laughed. Weiner brings an instant "auto-smile" to one's face. I see and hear a prankster, an entertainer, a comedian.

*I want to be a Kindergarten teacher, because they are little kids.*

Laughter and merrymaking is healthier than frowning and fretting. A smile brings on positive possibilities and makes us appear more approachable too. Turn that negative thought into a positive one. The more you practice, the better you'll feel.

Why did naturally curly-haired Devon, from Ms. Olenick's first grade class, return her book quick like lightning to the librarian? She had excitedly chosen the book *Where the Wild Things Are*, by Maurice Sendak, but it was written entirely in Spanish. "Excuse me, Mrs. Brogan," she faintly whispered, "I can't keep this book. I can't read Japanese."

Devon makes it very clear that she is honest and sincere. She will be an excellent and very devoted asset in human service relations. She may also become an internationally known Spanish or Japanese interpreter. Remember, one can have numerous professions. After all, we all are aware that women can multi-task.

The Kindergarten classes get so excited every February 2$^{nd}$. It is, of course, the official and traditional celebration of Groundhog's Day. "Why," you ask? It must be because their teacher, Ms. Kramer, brings her dog, Pebbles, to school. Pebbles is a purebred pug. Only the kindergarten classes celebrate Groundpug Day. All the kindergarten students with their teachers gather in the school playground, bundled in their polar fleece and puffy coats, as Ms. Kramer holds her permissive pug Pebbles toward the direction of the sun. If Pebbles sees her shadow, it means six more weeks of winter; if she does not see her shadow, it means an early spring. Next to Punxsutawney Phil, Pug Pebbles tells the true tale/tail.

*I want to be a professional basketball player, football player, and baseball player.*

These kids are revealing and expressing their love for animals. They are also honoring all groundhogs and pugs in Pennsylvania. Perhaps we may encounter our future dog breeders, trainers, groomers, or proud owners of "Pets R US." Pets are delightful additions to many families. A genuine dog, cat, horse, ferret, rabbit, chinchilla, bird, fish, hamster, guinea pig, or hermit crab owner would know.

How can David walk into the school library, complete with 6,769 books, including an additional 844 paperbacks, search for a book to sign out, taking a total of 15 minutes of his class period, reluctantly approach the librarian and announce to her, "I can't find any good books." A situation like this makes every hair on my body stand on edge and drives me near insanity.

Granted, there are numerous fairy tales with tiny fairies included, that could offer their precious time to magically appear and grant the true wish book to each and every child in the school. We could call on the lucky St. Patty's Day Leprechaun. Then, I'd regretfully be out of a job. Perhaps, children with David's caliber of charming character need fewer choices. Some children and adults (I admit I am one) have difficulty making decisions among the countless choices. We are very content with fewer items to choose from. We need a few basic items; food, clothing, shelter, pencil, pen, paper, and our inventive ideas to write about. I predict that David will write a few best-selling novels.

Just like when I was a kid, every Friday afternoon in kindergarten was "Show and Tell," followed by "Chat Time." Little Adam wanted to describe his new baby cousin Hannah to his classmates. The letter of the week was the letter *I*. Adam brought in a tube of *Cakemaker Icing*. "My cousin, her name is Hannah,

*I hope to make a CD and be a Music Award winner.*

is 8 weeks old," Adam said. "Last night, my mom told me she was swathed in her receiving blanket, but I think she was just wrapped. It was baby girl's pink colored, like cotton candy, or like those long-legged birds some people have in their front yards, and she was sleeping, out like a light, in her bassinet. When my cousin Hannah is sleeping, she looks like fluffy pink icing on a birthday cake, the same color as is this tube here I brought," he pointed.

Adam has imagination. His future awaits him employed as a landscape architect, designing attractive public parks, Ivy League college campuses and PGA golf courses. Kids are born with creativity and individual talents. Always have kids explore the possibilities, expand their horizons, share their gifts. Always encourage, never discourage. Make them feel proud. They will thank you one day.

Why did Patrick reluctantly participate in the "Flight of the Bumblebee" dance, head adorned with his "one of a kind" hand-made paper plate bee bonnet hat, antennae swirling and swaying as he walked? There were 27 black and yellow bumblebees happily dancing down the school hallway, imaginatively collecting pollen and nectar from flower to flower. "Come Follow Me" was the name of the song that was sung in a high-pitched volume. The "Queen Bee," their leader, asked Patrick about his obvious distress. Patrick held his ears tightly with his long antennae, his stinger tail shaking left and right. "Too loud" he replied, in his deep, monotone voice. "I'd rather be back at the hive eating honey."

Patrick's sweet tooth will grant him a scholarship to the finest culinary school, or continuous visits to his family dentist. Look for his exquisite confectionary shop on *Fifth Avenue*. Good Luck, Patrick!

If you thought girls were overbearing with their body spritzes, perfumes, hairsprays, mousse, flavored and scented lip glosses, and age-defying make-up, have you gotten a whiff of how the boys spray themselves these days?

*I want to be a movie star because I want to make a lot of money.*

P.U! They can overcome the girls, like smog overwhelms New York City. It is a very distinctive odor from the girls for sure! Lost in the shuffle (au revoir, adios, and arrivederci) with this generation of fragrances and masculine aromas are Aqua Velva, Brut, and Old Spice.

Carpooling each morning at 7:30 A.M. on pickup for middle school with three teenage boys, I have my car windows rolled down long before the boys stumble somberly into my car. The combination of scents that settle into my Subaru's upholstery can be compared to the blast that hits you when you drive into a Sunoco station smelling freshly spilled gasoline. "Oh, where is my surgeon's mask?" Boys must lure the girls, I presume. Convincing and coaxing personalities lead to tomorrow's corporate investigators, top-notch real estate agents, and select salesmen.

How many times have we heard kids say, "He cut!" or "She cut?" Cut what? Cut whom? Cut where? These phrases refer to someone unexpectedly leaping up in front of another kid in line.

"Jamie always cuts!"
"John cuts every day after gym class."
"That's not fair!"
"CUTTER,"
"You're a cutter!"
"Cutter, cutter, toss you in the gutter, you will start to stutter!" Remarks such as these are made.

This type of kid is driven and compulsively reacts. Jamie and John could be our future stunt car or NASCAR drivers, secret service agents, or a butcher, a baker, or a candlestick maker. Cut it out! Cut and dried! Cut through the red tape! Cutters automatically go to the back of the line!

*I want to be a cop.*

What is the meaning of the "bunny ear" thing that kids do with their two fingers (V) behind another kid's head? (Especially when a photograph is about to be taken) Who started that anyway? Does it have anything to do with sign language? A secret code? Was it an act of the 60's? or 50's? I think they will strive for peace in our world. May they become our ambassadors, our diplomats, and our peacemakers. Peace (V) be with those kids and peace be with you. Pray for peace on earth.

Five-year-old Matthew could not come to school on the original starting date of September 4th. A broken leg kept him home for the first six weeks. A cool autumn day in October blew Matthew into the parent drop-off back entrance of the school. Underlying jitters didn't hold him back from wearing his short-sleeved black T-shirt, with the heavy metal rock band on the front, *Kiss*. His husky designer blue jeans were a few sizes too big and were comfortably dragging on the floor, covering his sneakers. His hair was the color of burnt, desert tumbleweed, stray and wild. He cleared his throat and said to his teacher, "You can call me Matty. Where's my locker at?"(Hmmmmm? What's up with this young man? )

"Are you 'parent pick-up after school' or will you be taking the bus?" his teacher politely asked the young lad.

"No bus for me," Matty replied. "My brother, Vinnie, will get me. He's in 8th grade here. You remember him. He's six feet tall and has really big hair."

"Oh yes, I remember him very well," Mrs. Redwinski replied. "He seemed to be in the office rather frequently, probably helping the principal."

Siblings are so similar, yet so different in age. Matty, a younger version of Vinnie, truly looked up to his big brother. This twosome may follow in their father's footsteps as a heavy equipment manager or mechanic. Definitely, a dynamic duo.

*I want to be a crocodile hunter.*

# Chapter 2

## Kindergarten shares their positive thoughts

Here are a few of their responses.

- I don't know what positive is. "All right then Frankie, I said, tell me something good that happened to you today."

- O.K. I didn't pee my bed last night. Mom was real happy about that.

- I woke up at 20 o'clock.

- I had Cocoa Puffs with chocolate milk for breakfast.

- I almost tied my shoes all by myself. Mom and Dad promised me a new football when I can do it.

- I opened my locker all by myself!

- Look! I lost my toof!

- I got invited to Basil and Annie's birthday party. It's at Chuck E.Cheese's!

- My new puppy, Cleo, came in the car with me to school today. My old dog Razor died.

- I told my mom I'm done with school now. I went enuf times.

*I want to be a politician.*

- I watched my favorite TV show *Spongebob* before school today.

- I didn't fall out of my bed last night.

- My shoes! (jumping up and down) My Spiderman shoes light up red every time I move! LOOK! LOOK!

- I didn't get toothpaste on my shirt.

- I'm going to see my Dad over the weekend.

- Mia's coming to my house after school today.

- I ate Lucky Charms. It's going to be a good day.

- I hugged my kitten and my cat at 7:00 A.M.

- Carlene said she liked my ducky socks.

- Our Mommy lamb had a baby lamb in the night.

- I put my shoes on the right feet.

- I have money for the Book Fair today. I can buy two things, Mom said.

- I will not cry in the lunchroom today.

- Because my teacher said so, I have to share with Amanda.

- Tomorrow is my birthday. I get to wear "THE BIRTHDAY HAT" all day at school.

- I am thankful there are no mosquitoes in the winter.

*I want to be a scientist. When I am a scientist I want to dissect a frog.*

# Chapter 3

## Writers of First Grade relay what they would like to be when they grow up

- *Future Principal:* I am going to be a principal when I grow up. I will be working with the teachers. My school will have an elevator, four floors, one cafeteria, twelve classrooms, and one part of the school will be stairs. Oh, and the monkey bars are outside too. How many yards are at school? There are 50 yards of grass and a couple hills too. My school is almost as high as the Empire State Building.

- *Future Cop*: I want to be a cop when I grow up. I be chasing a guy who broke into a store and I will say, "Put your hands up!" If that didn't work I will chase him and chase him. When I catch him, I will put him in jail.

- *Future Inventor*: When I grow up, I want to be an inventor. I want to do this because I like inventing with the things in my crayon bag. The person I will be working with is Daniel. Hopefully, we will be a good team. I will be wearing old clothes because I might get dirty. I will need to live close by because I should not drive too far and Mom said she'd miss me.

- *Future Dancer*: When I grow up, I want to do this because you get to dance. The people I will be working with are nice. Hopefully I win! I will look good because I will wear a poofy pink dress with gloves to match. I will need to live in New York City because if I did not live there, I couldn't do the show.

*I want to be a marine biologist because I would like to be around sea animals.*

- *Future Hockey Player*: When I grow up I want to be a hockey player because it is fun. I get to skate and you play games some time too. I will look great because of my shirt because of the penguin on it.

- *Future Architect*: When I grow up I want to be an architect. I want to be this because I'm good at designing things. Hopefully my friends will want to be one too. I will look great because of my designing clothes. I will need to live in Pennsylvania because you can be an architect anywhere!

- *Future Hairdresser*: When I grow up, I want to be a hairdresser. I want to do this because my mom was a hairdresser. I will wear a cape and have sharp scissors to cut hair and I will fix my Nana's hair real nice.

- *Future Construction Worker*: When I grow up I want to be a construction worker. I want to do this because Pop does it. The people I will be working with are nice. Hopefully I will look great because I will wear orange with black straps and pants. I will need to live in a home with my family because me and my family would be homeless.

- *Future Chef*: When I grow up, I will wear black pants and a hat. I will need to live at a restaurant because I will make bread and muffins.

- *Future Star*: I want to be a star when I grow up. I will work on a stage. I will be singing. I want to be this because I like singing. I will be living in Hollywood and wearing a red dress. I will be working with other stars.

- *Future MLB Baseball player*: I want to be a baseball player when I grow up. I want to hit a home run so my brother Jayson can catch it in the grandstand.

- *Future Priest*: I want to be a priest in a really big church with fancy glass windows. They get paid a lot of money because of the baskets that are brought up to the altar every week.

*I want to be working anywhere with animals: bark, meow, and moo.*

# Chapter 4

## Writers of Second Grade relay what makes them happy

- My family makes me the happiest person of all people!

- Holidays.

- My dog makes me feel happy.

- School (Do you believe it?)

- My mom and dad, friends, school, family, food, shelter, holidays, Santa Claus, my cell phone and world peace.

- The winter makes me feel happy.

- Chocolate, homework, and the color purple.

- When Christmas, New Year's, Halloween, and Easter come up.

- If I could live in a mansion and be a princess.

- Tables, so we don't have to eat off the floor.

*I want to be a few things like a designer, a teacher, artist, singer, or own some kind of store.*

- If I could own a million puppies.

- Reading *Magic Tree House* books and *Ready Freddy* books.

- Money.

- The New York Giants make me the happiest.

- My kitten Bozo, Laffy Taffy and peanut M&M's, American girl dolls, Disney World and the Bahamas.

- Superheroes make me happy.

- Getting candy on Halloween makes me happy.

- Star Wars, playing the PS2, eating Snickers bars, presents, finding things I lost, chocolate milk, science, Easter, no homework, money, and bottle cap collecting.

- Root beer, wrestling and The United States of America rock!!!!!!!

- Playing cars in my back yard. Being at my home with Mom and Dad. Watching TV and eating fries, nachos, cheeseburgers, and drinking Brisk iced tea.

- Shopping at Toys R Us, and eating my birthday cake.

- When I get a new tie.

- Saturday and Sunday.

- Money, because I want to be retch.

- My dog, Max.

- Rainbows, flowers, my computer and my friends.

- Candy, ice cream, money, flat screen TV, food, Game Cube, school, friends, bubble gum, (the best is Big League Chew) U.S.A., my MP3 player, apple juice, and cowboys make me happy.

*I want to be a Strong Safety for the Dallas Cowboys.*
*What you do is you line up behind the*
*Linebackers then you tackle the player with the ball.*

- Snow, games, my mom, school, my teacher, my friends, my family, and going to the Dominican Republic make me happy.

- Chocolate milk and Oreo cookies.

- My PS3, PS2, and my Gameboy, and my tons of games, wrestling and basketball and baseball and football, and not school. Not math either, and I like TV too.

- Winning the coloring contest in the newspaper.

- Going to McDonald's for a milk shake.

- Seeing my baby sister when I get home from school.

- When we have a snow day.

- When we have a ice day.

*I want to be a Professional soccer player.*

# Chapter 5

## Writers of Third Grade share their favorite book

- My favorite book is *A Series of Unfortunate Events*, by Lemony Snicket. It's the ninth book in the series and it's very interesting. He is a good author and illustrator. I wonder how the book ends? I could just go to the back of the book and see, but then I won't know how the middle is.

- My favorite book is *Spiderman 2*. The reason why I like this book is because I really enjoy Spiderman and I enjoy reading about Spiderman and I have a whole shelf of Spiderman and I really like Spiderman.

- My favorite book is *Derek Jeter*. The reason why I like this book is because I like to watch baseball. Derek Jeter is my favorite player on the New York Yankees. Derek Jeter has a lot of home runs. He is a fast runner. Derek Jeter almost looks like my uncle. If you people want to read about Derek Jeter, you can get lots of books about him.

- My favorite book is *Harry Potter and the Prisoner of Azkaban*. I really enjoy reading Harry Potter books. I think it is a good experience. If you like adventure I recommend this book. And also if you like chapter books this would be a good book for you. Some of them are thick and some are not. Some are scary, but to me they are not.

*I want to be an archeologist that works on the History Channel.*

- My favorite book is *Each Little Bird That Sings*. It has many details to help me understand about people you love dying. It was a very sad book and it was very interesting.

- My favorite book is *The Very Hungry Caterpillar*. I like it because it tells you about how a caterpillar eats and how it forms into a butterfly. That is my short report.

- My favorite book is *Juliet Low, Girl Scout Founder*. I like this book because I like girl scouts and it is good for other girl scouts. It could also get more girls to join Girl Scout troops around the globe. I also love the book because it has a lot about the past in girl scouting. The book taught me more about girl scouting than anything else. Now I know everything about girl scouts and it gave me more knowledge with girl scouting.

- My favorite book is *The Philadelphia Eagles*. I like this book because I love football. The Philadelphia Eagles are my favorite team in NFL history. The Eagles have won only one Super Bowl in their history. They went to three Super Bowls, but they lost two and won one. In 1964, the Eagles were the best team in NFL. The next year the Eagles did not make it to the playoffs because they did not play their hardest. I have an Eagles hat and jacket.

- My favorite book is *Girls and their Horses*. The reason I like this book is it teaches you tips about horses. I enjoyed seeing how you take care of horses and it teaches you all kinds of tricks people could do on them. People could stand on top of each others shoulders on a horse which I think is neat!

- My favorite book is *Strawberry Shortcake*. The book smells like strawberries and she has a lot of friends and my aunt Marisa has the whole collection of Strawberry Shortcake dolls from when she was little.

- My favorite book is *High School Musical*. The reason why I like this book is because I've seen the movie so many times. I wanted to see if anything was different. I enjoyed reading it because my friend and I were reading the book at the same time. It was fun to see who would get done first. My friend Wendy got done before me. It was a good book!

*I want to be a pizza maker.*

- My favorite book is *Helen Keller* because it was interesting learning about a blind and deaf girl. I liked reading Chapter 3, it was my favorite part. It taught me sign language. At home I have *Helen Keller* the first addition. Well no matter what Helen Keller book she wrote, I like them all. And I loved the ending; it was great. And when I finished the book, I knew more about Helen Keller.

- *Ralph S. Mouse* is my favorite book because Ralph is my name and it was funny.

- My favorite book is called *Ronald Reagan*. It is very interesting and it is about a very good person, and because he was a very good president. I wish I would have been alive when he was the president. I think that he was the best president ever. I wish he was still alive. He was the best. Even though some people don't like him, I know I do.

- My favorite books are the *Goosebumps* series. I really like scary stuff and there is a lot of scary stuff in these books, and I love mysteries.

- *Baked Beans for Breakfast* was a very interesting book. It felt like you were in the book. It did take me a long time to read it but it still would have to be my favorite book. I also liked it because just about everyone in the book is my age.

- My favorite book is *Harold and the Purple Crayon*. I like to draw like Harold does.

- My favorite book is *Flat Stanley*. It's about a nice boy who went to the doctor. Everything was going fine until a billboard dropped on his head. He is a half an inch thick now. Stanley can do neat tricks such as folding and mailing himself to Ohio and sliding underneath doors. He can also turn into a kite. I would recommend this book to anyone who likes chapter books that are fun.

- My favorite book is *I Wonder Why Pyramids Were Built*. I felt like I was in the first century. Some of this century I found interesting. Sometimes I found it gross. I like the part where they have outside meetings. Sometimes they meet in certain places. I would not recommend this book to girls. I think boys would be more interested in it.

*I want to be a Sea World worker.*

# Chapter 6

**Writers of Fourth Grade were asked:
If you could name a new star or planet,
what would you name it and why?**

- If I had to name a star, I would name it *SPARKLE*. Because at night I like to watch it shine in the sky and glitter at the same time and it looks beautiful. If I could see a star and name it I would come outside every night and watch it. At nighttime I love to look at the stars in the sky twinkle and glitter.

- I would name my planet *THOMAS ALLEN* because two of my grandfathers are named Thomas and Allen. They also fought in the war but died of old age and it means a lot to me. Also because my dad's name is Thomas too.

- I would name my planet *COBY*. I like that name. It's my dog's name. I love him.

- I would name my planet *SINCO*. It is 300 degrees F and the population is very low. The only kind of things that could live on the planet is lizards because of the extreme temperatures.

- I would name it *THOR* because of the massive electrical storms that cover the surface of the planet. THOR was the Norse God of thunder. The planet Thor circles a distant star 25,000 light years from Earth. Its size is five times

*I want to be a NASCAR driver and a carpenter because
I like to drive things and I like to build things.*

that of earth. THOR takes three earth years to complete one orbit of its star. The atmosphere of THOR is composed mainly of neon gas. The electrical storms cause the gas to glow giving the planet an orangish colored sky in which there is 6 moons. The surface of the planet is over 400 degrees F. Life as we know it on earth is not found on the planet THOR.

- I would name it *KESTOS* and I don't have a reason.

- I would name a new planet *MOONBEAN* because it could be by the moon and be shaped like a bean. The color of Moonbean would be green.

- I would name my planet *MOOCOW*. It would be inhabited by moocows and ruled by a pig.

- I would name a planet *SPORTSTOPIA*. On it would be all the different sports in the world on a list. You would need the list to find the equipment of the sport that you were looking for. The planet would be 15 times bigger than the earth. Also on the planet would be tips, secrets, and how to play the different sports. There would also be training rooms with the best trained professionals to teach you. That is what my planet will be like.

- If I found a star I would name it the *MONKAPHANT STAR*. It would be a mix of an elephant and a monkey, and those are my two favorite animals. I named it that because I'm the founder of this planet, so I should get to name it whatever I want.

- If I could name a new planet I would name it *PLANET SOCCERBALL*. It would look like a giant soccer ball. On planet Soccerball everyone that lived there would have a soccer ball head. Since your head would be a soccer ball, you can take it off and a new one would grow back right away. If you take off your head that means you get to kick it around. That is what I would name my planet.

- I would name my planet *KARATATARA*. Karat stands for karate, and Tara stands for the founder's name, ME. I like karate!

- *ZEEGWAX TURTLE LAND*. I would name it that because I like turtles and because Zeegwax sounds cool.

*I want to be a Crime Scene Investigator for the CSI.*

- If I found a new planet, I would name it *PLANET FOFO*. It would be an all-girl planet. It is pink with white swirls. It would have rings that are light blue. There would be 500 active volcanoes that spewed light blue cotton candy all day long.

- If I named a planet I would name it *THE SOCCERMATIC* because it would be a big blue soccer ball with brown spots. I love soccer and Matic would be the founder of the planet. If you fly to this planet there is a big soccer field with aliens playing soccer on it. Whatever team won would rule it until the next game but they are not allowed to do anything mean or bad. When my planet rotates around 300 times, their fathers and mothers will call them to come and eat. This will happen every time it rotates around 300 times. This is why I would call it the Soccermatic.

- I would name a planet *ERASER* because people there make lots of mistakes. The planet would be pink, blue, red, white and green. It would also have ten moons because I am ten. The moons names would be Pencil, Book, Math, Hockey, Pen, Paper, Test, Glue, Map and School. It would have a blue sun.

- I would name a new planet *HAMMY*. I would name it this because the planet that I found looks like a hamster. Also Hammy, the word, reminds me of hamsters. The planet is white and has a little black thing where an eye would go. It would be fuzzy too.

- I would name a planet *TURTLEZORPH* because it would be home to many alien turtles. Alien turtles can stand up and run. I would discover it.

- If I could name a planet, I would name it *PLANET HERSHEY* because it would be made out of chocolate. It would be a brand new flavor of chocolate. The flavor would be (CVS) chocolate vanilla sherbet.

- I would name my planet *J*. Because all over the planet is the gigantic letter J and it is the shape of a J. My name is Jared.

- My planet would be named *WISHADINGADONG* because it's a funny name and it would make everyone laugh.

- If I could name a planet I would name it *PLANET BASKETBALL* because the planet would be orange with black stripes just like a basketball. It would

*I want to be a ROCKSTAR.*

rain orange and black raindrops, and it would snow basketballs. Everyone that lived there had to have a basketball hoop to play or wait for it to snow again. Also, everyone will be having so much fun on the planet that they will live forever. You could eat the basketballs because if you don't there will be too many, and they taste like whatever candy you are thinking of at the time.

- My planet would be called *HORSEHAVEN* because I love horses. My family has horses and horses are awesome to ride. The horses there would run free and they would be able to breathe and there's lots of grass and water for them to eat and drink. People will also live on the planet and they would make everything for horses. There would be barns, houses, fences and other things, so many things can live in the planet. People would make horse treats, horse medicine, and horse food. They would make hay and there would be so much grass and flowers on the ground for them. There would be horse tracks and stables. You wouldn't have to pay for the horses because you take care of them. No horses will be left behind.

- *MICKEY* would be the name of my planet. I would name it Mickey because they found out Pluto is a moon for a planet, so since Pluto is the dog for Mickey Mouse, I would name it Mickey. It would be a red planet.

- I would name my star *DREAMER* because it twinkles in the night sky. And because it is always sparkling and people like to look up to a star and dream for things that they need or want to get. It would also have a small shooting star with a colorful ending.

- If I could name a planet it would be called *PLANET CATS* because my favorite animal is a cat. It would also be for all lost cats. It would have rolly polie balls, canned cat food, comfortable places to sleep, and lots of warm milk. It would be a cat's paradise.

- My planet would be called *GIRLSRULEIT.* No boys allowed! Only when they buy a ticket for Boysday are they allowed to come.

*I want to be a farmer.*

# Chapter 7

**Writers of Fifth Grade were asked: If you could visit any place in the world, where would you visit and why?**

- I want to go to the Great Barrier Reef Marine Park. There are many animals there. There is more than 1,500 species of fish! There's 30 species of marine mammals. There's 5,000 species of mollusk. I love sea animals!

- If I were to go somewhere I would go to Hawaii. Where would you go? It is so nice out there! The palm trees are so neat. I have never been on a plane, but I think it would be fine. I wouldn't have to worry about the snow. It has beaches so I could go swimming. There are dolphins and I love dolphins! That's why I picked Hawaii.

- If I could pick a place to go to I would go to Knoxville, Tennessee. I go there often now because I have relatives there. I would also like to play football at the University of Tennessee. I would also like to go there because it is hot in the summer and when it is winter, it snows but it is not that cold all winter.

- If I could visit my favorite place I would already be there. My place is Long Island. Most of my family lives there and I love visiting them! I miss my old home and friends, school and teachers. My family is very nice. My aunts, uncles, brother and sister are very good to me. I love the parks and beaches they have! In the summer I go with my cousins to their school and play at the playground sometimes. It is so fun at Long Island! When I go to Long

*I want to be a zookeeper.*

Island, I sleep over my cousin's house. It's fun when my cousins and I stay up and play. The sunsets on the beaches are so beautiful! If I could I would choose Long Island. I forgot to tell you, it's in New York. Long Island is my favorite place.

- I would like to go to Daytona Beach, Florida. The weather is great all year long and the Daytona 500 is there. I would also like to go there because you could catch really big fish and it's not far from some of my relatives, but I mostly want to go there because of the beach.

- I'd travel to England because I have always wondered what it looked like. I always thought it would be a beautiful place to visit. Another reason is that Paul McCartney lived there. Paul McCartney is my favorite singer in the world! He is better than a snow day on the day you are to have a big test! Those are some of the reasons why I would go to England. Do you know where you would go?

- I would pick Paris to visit to learn the French language. That way I could understand what people who speak this language are saying. Another reason is I would like to go shopping in Paris, to see the different styles this country has from America. Also, I hear the tours that the hosts give are fantastic; they show you everything. Did you ever dream of seeing the extravagant Eiffel Tower? It is a known landmark in Paris, France. It is all lit up with beautiful white lights. Also, I heard they have great food except for those cooked salted snails they make there. That is the country I would like to visit someday soon.

- Hawaii. My aunt used to live there for many years. She told me that when she would wake up every morning she could smell the saltwater from the ocean. My aunt also said that she would drink the milk out of coconuts. The climate, even in the winter time is always extremely warm!!! The way the Hawaiian people dress is awesome because of their grass skirts and coconut tops. My aunt also said that the people of Hawaii are very friendly. All of these things are the reason why this is the place in the world that I would love to go.

- I chose Hawaii because there is no winter and I will go swimming. My grandma will sit in the sun, my grandpa will fish, and my brother will sit in the house all day long and watch television.

- If I had a choice to go somewhere, I would go to Miami, Florida. My favorite NBA team is there and I would go swimming for 2 hours and then I would go fishing. I would go scuba diving and go crabbing and after that I'll eat all that stuff.

*I want to be a traveler.*

- I would go to Italy because of the great structures like the Leaning Tower of Pisa and the Coliseum. I like the boot shape of Italy. Italy is the coolest country. My favorite thing about Italy is Venice. All the places are very nice and the Gondolas are neat. I cannot forget the Italian food like pizza or spaghetti and Italian bread. I love Italian food.

- I would like to visit Russia because of their unexplored land. If I find the unexplored land, I probably would become rich and famous. If I became famous and rich I could help my family. My mom for example, spends all her money on flowers. If I get the money, I will buy her some every day. I will give some money to my uncle so he can spend more money on my baby cousin Dillon. I will put the rest of my money to my band, The Rebels, to get better equipment like amps, microphones, guitars and drums.

- I would pick to go to Dallas, Texas because it's awesome there! There are many things to do down in Dallas. First, I would get some hot wings. Second, I would go see a Dallas Cowboys game, and I would take my dad. Third, I would take my grandfather to go hunting outside the city of Dallas for some nice deer. And finally, I would go down to Dallas so I could enjoy some peace and quiet without my sister Shannon.

- I would go to Hawaii because it is never too hot or cold; well maybe sometimes too hot. You could see the pretty palm trees that are hard as a big red brick. You could dive in the nice cool ocean. You could surf and go fishing, but don't catch a shark. The pretty sea is as blue as the sky without clouds. I could see how nice the hotels are. If you could not understand what people were saying ask them to teach you to speak their way. If you wanted to buy a surfboard you could buy one at a surf shop. You could probably ride your quad in the woods. It would be fun to scuba dive in the deep blue sea. It would be cool to see the bright colors on some of the fish that stay in the deep blue sea. If I went scuba diving I would be careful that a shark doesn't see me. If a shark attacked you, you would be dead. You can swim fast if a shark was following you.

- If I could visit any place in the world I would go to Germany because that is where my family came from. I also always wanted to see the castles and visit Berlin and see the Berlin Wall. I would like to learn the language and look for my other relatives too. On the way back to America, I would also want to visit Normandy Beach.

*I want to be a fashion designer.*

- I would go to Assateague Island and I know that you are wondering why. I adore horses. They deserve to run free and not be kept in their stalls all day long. They are living, breathing creatures just like you and me. Horses are as beautiful as butterflies! They come in all colors, sizes, and shapes! They are all special in their own ways. At Assateague, the horses roam around free. Another reason I would like to go there is that the scenery is serene. The moors and beaches blend together to make the most beautiful and natural wilderness you could ever see. If I ever had a chance to go to Assateague, I'd accept it in a heartbeat! I hope my dream will come true!

- I would go to the Bermuda Triangle because it's a mysterious place. People, aircraft, boats and U.S. battleships disappear in the Bermuda Triangle and they were never found. Some people think these things disappear because of the weather patterns. Only one person ever came out of the Bermuda Triangle alive! I want to see if the myth of the Bermuda Triangle is true. That's where I want to go.

- I know where I would go; I'd go to Dallas, Texas because of two things. Number 1) to go to see the Dallas Cowboys, (my favorite football team) and 2) I love Texan sizzled steak. Texan sizzled steak is probably about the best steak there is! It is juicy, and it is cooked on a grill over a fire made of coal and wood. You probably have a different place than me that you would like to go. I go for Dallas, Texas.

- If I had the chance to go anywhere in the world, I would definitely go to Miami, Florida. I would go there for the nice weather. I would go for the swimming. The main reason I would go there is for the Miami Heat. I've always liked Shaquille O'Neal. I like Jason Williams, Dwayne Wade and Alonzo Mourning. So when they put those four on the Miami Heat, the Heat instantly became my favorite basketball team and I've always wanted to see a Heat game.

- Imagine you are on a popular game show, and you were trying to win a trip to your favorite destination. Where would you choose? I would choose Kingston, Jamaica. The first reason is they have lots of coffee, and I love coffee! Also each U.S. dollar is worth about 47 Jamaican dollars, so I would be rich! Finally, I would choose Jamaica because of the average temperature. It is 84 degrees. I would come home with a tan! Those are the reasons why I would like to win a trip to Kingston, Jamaica. Oh yeah, one more question. Any ideas how I would get on that game show?

*I want to be a children's book artist or a professional cook, because I love to draw and I love to cook.*

- I'll move to Montana and own my own horse ranch. I will live in a big log cabin and gaze out the window and see snow covered mountains, an eagle flying overhead, the smell of pine trees. I want to go to Montana.

- I would visit Wildwood, New Jersey and go on the Splash Zone. Splash Zone is a water park with a 50 gallon bucket at the top. When filled the bucket tilts over and the water lands on the swimmers below in the pool. I want to go deep sea fishing there too. I want to go on a boat just for one day and catch salt water fish.

- Washington D.C. because I want to see the Washington monument and the White House, other National Monuments and our first flag, because it was just restored.

- I would want to go to Australia right now, because it's the greatest place to see the best animals like the kangaroo, because they're so hip-hoppy. The koala is cool because all you have to do to go to sleep is just find a nice tree. There are also wombats and Tasmanian wolves that live there but the Tasmanian wolves are now extinct. Yup. I would sure want to be in Australia right now, plus I'd do anything to escape this cold weather.

- I agree, Australia is the place for me. I always wanted to go there. Australia is where Steve Erwin was born and the accent there is cool. It's like "Elo there chum" and there are a lot of different animals to see and catch. There are many birds to watch and catch in the sky and the sky is super clear, hardly a cloud in sight, at night stars glitter like a moons reflection in a mirror. That is why I would want to go to Australia. "See you chum!"

- Disney World because all kids love to have fun and all kids watch the Disney Channel.

- I want to go visit my Aunt in Hawaii, but my Mom is afraid to fly there. She mails me and my brother neat stuff, macadamia bead necklaces, key chains, a shark's tooth, good luck charms, and once she sent us a can of Spam. I didn't know what that was. She loves living there and someday I will get to see her again. Aloha!

- If I could visit any place in the world I would go to Ireland. Irish people are the happiest people and they really like to eat and be merry. The four-leaf clovers there are as green as the grass. When you celebrate your birthday, they bounce you on your head for every year you are!

*I want to be an Art teacher. Because I love art!*

- I would pick the countryside. I could ride my horse Jinny and have a campout at the streams. I would learn how to milk cows and goats. There are nice fields of grass that look like the wide open sea. I would live on a nice farm with cows, horses, sheep, dogs, cats, fish, pigs, chickens, mice, rabbits, snakes, spiders, and a lot of people to work with to help take care of them.

*I want to be a War Flying Ace.*

# Chapter 8

**Writers of Sixth Grade were asked this question: Name someone who has inspired you and why? It could be a member of your family, a friend, or other**

- Someone who inspired me was my mom. She helped me get over my fear of heights.

- My father has inspired me because he always taught me not to give up. He taught me the sport of baseball and most of his family love "baseball." Hopefully I will become a baseball player just like my father always wanted me and my brother to be.

- Someone who has inspired me is my sister Sarah. She does because she is very nice and she drives me to friend's houses. She even cooks for me and my other sister, mom, and stepdad, Mr. Mike. She inspires me because she's the greatest sister ever. She's nice to me and gives me gum and Jolly Ranchers! Those are the reasons why I think Sarah inspires me and I love her so much!

- Someone who has inspired me is my mom. My mom is great, she is always happy. She always takes care of me whenever I am sick. She does all my laundry and cooks me dinner. My mom takes me shopping and to tons of cool places. She teaches me how to cook and she teaches me a lot about fashion. I love my mom so much I wish I could be just like her when I am older.

*I want to be a Penn State football player!!*

- Someone who has inspired me is my mom and dad. They helped me be who I am today. My dad helped me do sports and my mom helped me have manners. My mom helped me be a better person. My dad helped me go outside, before that I hated outdoors and my dad helped me to learn to swim. My dad buys food for me and makes it, cleans my clothes, and helps me out when I am hurt. I want to be like my mom and dad when I grow up.

- The person that inspired me is Chriss Angel. He inspires me because I want to learn how to do tricks like him. Some of the tricks he does are like cut a lady in half. He is really cool! He has a show called *Chriss Angel Mind Freak*. It is on every Wednesday.

- My dad inspires me. He teaches me magic tricks, basketball moves, and makes the best pizza.

- I am inspired by Travis Pastrana. He is the first and youngest kid to be a dirt bike superstar. I want to be the second person. Also Travis is the first one to do a double back flip. I am a good dirt bike rider but not as good as him.

- Someone who has inspired me is my mom. My mom told me to start ice skating. And if my mom did not tell me to start, I would not be where I'm at today. Thanks, Mom.

- There are many people who inspire me in my life. If I had to choose one, it would be my sister Allyson. She's smart and funny. I would want to be just like her when I'm older. Sometimes we don't get along, but when we do its fun. When I don't know something she will help me. It's great having an older sister. It's not the best when we fight, but we usually get along pretty good. So although we fight, she is still the one that inspires me the most.

- I was inspired by Tiger Woods to play golf. I am playing now and I own many items from his biographies. He is my favorite golfer. I am hoping to be as good as him some day. I even already have clubs, balls, a bag, markers, tees, divot replacers, golf journal, and other things. I really love to play this sport!

- Many people have inspired me in my life as I grow older. But there always was one person who inspires me still to this day, and always will is my sister Brynne. Even though she is stubborn and doesn't always follow the

*I want to be an N.F.L. wide receiver because I like football.*

rules she has accomplished many things. Already in High School, she has always gotten straight A's and had the opportunity to go to Washington, D.C. for The National Young Leaders Conference. She has also been in the National Junior Honor Society for two years. She runs track and plays soccer. Everything that I have stated is why I picked my sister as my inspiration and I hope I accomplish that much when I am her age.

- Someone who has inspired me is my mom. She has inspired me in different ways. One of those ways is that she showed me it takes hard work to do anything. She worked hard, and studied all through high school and college. My mom majored in computers and has a great job now. Also, she worked very hard in swimming. She trained a lot in her spare time and finally became a lifeguard. My mom has taught me that I can do anything that I want to do, as long as I work hard and try. That is how she's inspired me.

- I most admire Rosa Parks. I admire her most because she was so determined when she boycotted the buses for the African Americans. Even when the people jailed her, she didn't give up. It was just her stubborn and determined personality that I admire. I don't think I could ever go through what she went through. I also envy her patience. She walked for a long time and I can't imagine the hardships she faced just trying to walk miles from work to home. That is why I admire Rosa Parks.

- My grandmother inspired me with her love, her stubbornness, and her caring for the creatures we don't understand. She inspired me to be a veterinarian. My grandmother wasn't a vet but I always thought she was one. She always cared about animals but still had time for family. My grandma had herds of goats, cages full of dogs, one big mean pig, and a whole mess of cats running around. Yet she didn't let one in the house, they were all tame enough to pet. Yes, my grandma inspired me to be a veterinarian and that's what I'll be.

- My mother is a hard working person. She works really hard at her job. She also volunteers often. She volunteered to be the homeroom coordinator, and to become the Assistant leader of my Girl Scout Troop. Another example she sets is she doesn't drink, smoke or take drugs. She doesn't do that because she knows that it's bad, and she wants to be sure that we don't smoke, drink alcohol, or take drugs. She is also inspiring because you can talk to her, and she listens. Also I think she is very great role model, which means she is the most inspiring person I know.

*I want to be a gymnast in the Olympics.*

- My inspiration is my mom because she is always encouraging and does so many things for our family. She works, cooks and cleans. My mom has always told me to do my best at everything I choose to do. She has been to all of my dance recitals, cheerleading events, talent shows and school programs. She will always be special and she inspires me to be a good person, and to be whatever I want to be.

- The person who inspires me the most would be my mom. A few years ago she went back to school to be a dental hygienist. She also took care of my brother and me. She showed me that if you work hard at something, you will succeed. She worked hard at school, took care of us, and now she is a dental hygienist. That also showed me that hard work pays off. My mom taught me that I will succeed.

- My sister inspired me to dance. I was trying and trying hard to learn a new trick, but I just couldn't do it. She decided to help me and spot me when I tried. I did it a few times with her and it was good. Then I went to do it again. This time when I did it, I kicked her in the face. She didn't want to spot me anymore after that. Then she told me, "If you keep pushing hard at practice you'll be able to do it in no time. Just keep trying and pushing harder and harder." I listened to what she told me and eventually I was able to do the trick.

- Only one person has inspired me to do something that I carry out almost everyday. That person, without a doubt is my eldest brother Andrew. It all started about four years ago. My brother was soon to start a grueling basic training at the United States Military Academy or West Point. Even before he started his first day he was already an inspiration. He and his fellow cadets were the first class to respond to the call of duty after the 9/11 tragedy. He knew well that a war was imminent, yet he still proceeded. Andrew inspired to be brave under any circumstances. He had one last chance to quit without having to give any years of service three years after that day. Andrew did not choose the easy way out. He inspired me to never back away from any fear. Andrew has graduated from West Point and is now taking basic officer training. While I am writing this report, President George W. Bush is preparing to give a speech on what to do next in Iraq. In the coming months Andrew could possibly be deployed. I am comforted by knowing that wherever he may be, he will always be the greatest inspiration I have ever had.

- My dad is my biggest inspiration. He is loyal, caring, loves baseball, and he is very smart. My dad is loyal because whenever he says that he is going

*I want to be a video game creator.*

to do something, he follows up on what he says. He cares a lot about other people, not only himself like most people. He loves baseball which helps me a lot because whenever it is nice outside he pushes that we get outside and throw a baseball. My dad also makes the grounders, line drives, and pop-ups harder for me to catch as my skills improve. He is very smart so when I am having trouble with something, I can always go to him for help. I don't only see my dad because most of the time I think of him as my friend. This is why I chose my dad as the person who inspires me the most.

- The two people that inspire me the most are my Mom and Dad. They inspire me because when I moved to Drums, Pennsylvania, they only had soccer in the fall. In my old town they had it in the spring and in the fall. Here they have baseball in the spring. I wasn't going to sign up for baseball but my Mom and Dad convinced me to sign up for it so I did. When I tried out, I was good enough to play in Little League.

  Another time I didn't want to go out for soccer because I didn't know anyone around here. My Mom and Dad told me to try out for soccer and I did, and guess what? I knew two other boys there. One of the kids was in my third grade class. Once again, they inspired me. The last thing I didn't want to do was to go to the fishing derby at Beech Mountain Lakes. My Mom, Dad, and my Uncle Bob all convinced me to go to it. I didn't catch any, but the following year I caught three fish. Those are my reasons why my Mom and Dad both inspire me a lot.

- I am writing about how my dad inspired me to play basketball. When I played my first game, I loved it. He taught me more rules of the game, and he taught me how to shoot. Two years later I could make a three point shot. After three years, I perfected my foul shot. I continued to play in a league for four years.

- My dad inspires me the most. He is pretty much the leader of our family because he makes the decisions that we mostly do. He is also the one who taught me how to play things like basketball and soccer. When I was young, he taught me how to dribble, shoot, and pass a basketball and a soccer ball. He also showed me how to put stuff together like hooking up my television to my wall. One thing that is amazing about him is he can cook good meals. If anything would ever happen to my mom, my dad would do the best to replace her and be our dad at the same time. That is why my dad inspires me.

*I want to be a pet shop owner because I love to play with animals.*

- A person who has inspired me is my dad. I think that is because he is a hard worker, he is friendly, and he gets to travel many places. He is a district manager of Cracker Barrel, and many employees know him well. He motivates me to dream of the job I hope to have, a Nintendo game designer. He also has many qualities I am hoping to obtain, being a hard worker, being neat, and being kind. He earns a good salary too. Because of that, he can afford good clothing, food, and occasional vacations. Lastly, he always tries to be as helpful as possible. And that is why my Dad inspires me.

- Many people have inspired me in my life. I have learned many things from inspiring people. I would not be successful without these people, but there is someone who I think inspired me the most. My grandfather, Thomas Addes, was there for me every day. He was my mom's father. He taught me many things about life that have helped me. My grandfather served in the Navy during WWII. This was his dream. He followed his dreams and was very successful. When he told that story to me, he inspired me. Now I know how successful you will be if you follow your dreams. He inspired me to stand up for myself. It makes me who I am. My grandfather just wasn't a help to me, he was an inspiration to my brother Matt too.

- My inspiration is Mom because she is caring, loving, and patient. I don't have much patience, especially when it comes to my little brother! She can handle him when he's hyper; when I yell at him and chase him. (This does not help much) She has always been a great mom and always will be!

- Someone who inspires me is my 3$^{rd}$ grade teacher, Mrs. Bean. She always encouraged me and forced me to do things even when I didn't want to. She brought me out of my shell and guided me when I was completely lost. She is truly an inspiration to me.

- Someone who inspired me was my grandfather. He taught me about guns and hunting. He showed me what and where I could hunt when I got my hunting license. He also showed me how to set two different traps. What I want to hunt is a bobcat. If I get one, I'll see if I could stuff it, and use it as a trophy. My grandfather and I are also very alike. He taught me about World War II and we both watch a TV show about it, and we are both named Harry. He inspired me to hunt. Hopefully, I will get a bobcat when I get older.

- I am inspired by my first grade teacher, Mrs. Cain. She is a great teacher and friend. She inspired me to read. She would always read Junie B. Jones

*I want to be a bond trader because I like money and a soccer player on the weekends.*

books out loud to us. Those were the first books I have ever read. She also taught me to be a good person, to make new friends and to treasure old ones. She is my inspiration. She is my hero.

- My mom has inspired me to do anything my heart tells me to do. (As long as you know that it is not something bad.) She has said before that with the right attitude and brain power, anyone can change the world; you just have to work at it. My mom has also taught me to never give up, and I guess that I wouldn't be at MMI or where I am now if it wasn't for her.

- Two teachers are my inspiration who teach the classes of autistic students in my school, Mrs. Black and Miss Matulevich. Patience and a million times patience is their gift. A simple sound, reaction, recognition, or interaction among these special needs children adds another gift to their daily lessons.

*I want to be a Famous Fashion Designer.*

# Chapter 9

**Writers of Seventh Grade were asked—
What or who is the most amazing person,
time, place, or thing you have ever seen?**

- My sister is the most amazing person I've ever seen, since she saved my life and my family's life from a house fire.

- My dad is the most amazing person I know because he is a doctor who works very hard every day to make sick people better.

- I once saw two black bears in the back of my yard. My mom told me to point the flashlight on the bear and I did. Then my mom yelled, "Look Brad! There's another one!" I said, "Calm down, Mom, we are in the house."

- Once I went to the Grand Canyon. It was in Arizona. I saw the Northern Lights. They were beautiful. They were like nothing I had ever seen before. That was the most amazing thing I have ever seen.

- The most amazing thing I have ever seen was a concert at Penns Peak. I was up front and I saw all the lights, the band members, and I heard the loud amplifiers. After the concert, I met the band; I got a shirt with their signatures on it. That was the most awesome concert ever, and I hope to see them again. I really liked it, and it changed my life.

*I want to be an archeologist.*

- The most amazing thing I have ever seen was when me and my dad went fishing at a derby and I said that I wanted to get a big fish and I was only catching small fish and when I was waiting for a fish I saw a big fish in the lake. I told my Dad to get the net and I went right up to the water. I caught him but I could barely pick him up so my dad came to help me and we caught the fish and we put it in a bucket and we brought it up to the judges and they said that we had won and we got a brand new trophy and when we got home we put the fish in the oven and we ate it and it was the best fish we ever had for dinner.

- I saw the band Pink Floyd, 3 Doors Down, and Breakin Benjamin concerts. It was amazing! We got front row seats. It was so cool with all the super loud music, lights and screaming fans, you practically forgot your name. The down side was you could barely hear for three days. There were so many people that some people had to sit on other peoples shoulders. At the Pink Floyd concert, they threw twenty dollar bills and me and my dad each caught one. Finally, when we were leaving we got the money signed and our shirts too! The hardest part was when you had to get out of the parking lot. That was one of the most amazing times I have ever had.

- The most amazing person I ever saw was Isaac Bruce, a wide receiver for the St. Louis Rams. A lot of people say he stinks because he is in his twelfth season, but I think he rocks! I started liking him from one game I saw, and since then I loved him. It is weird being about one of about five people in the school who likes his team. When I wear the jersey, people say something about the Eagles or the Giants. What is really unique though, we have the same birthday. Even though some people don't like the Rams and Isaac Bruce, I still do.

- The most amazing person I have ever seen is Hillary Clinton. She is running for President of the United States. If she wins the election, she would be the first female President. I believe she would be a great President. I also believe she would change and touch people's lives. She has a very strong opinion. I think she will win the election and become President.

- The most amazing thing I have ever seen was the Eagles in the Super Bowl! Even though they lost, we had a great time. I hope to play for their team, meet all of the players, and win the Super Bowl. I hope to become a famous linebacker. I will be put in the Hall of Fame for everyone to see my picture. I will be great. I like the Eagles and would love to play for them. The Eagles at the Super Bowl was great and it was the most amazing thing I have ever seen.

*I want to be a wolf expert.*

- The most amazing person I have ever seen is my Nana's foster child, Judy. Judy is amazing because with all she's been through, she still has fun and is a wonderful child. She'll wish on a penny and throw it in a well and every time she will wish the same thing, "I wish I could go back to my Mommy." Even though she loves us dearly, she like every other foster child wants her mom back. She has been through therapy and many new families,
yet she acts like a member of our family. She sometimes calls my mom, Mommy and dad, Daddy. She loves my dad. Her mom made a few bad choices in her life, and her sister went through some tough times too, but she still sees the bright side of everything. She looks up to me, but she is a role model for me, more than she can imagine.

- The most amazing place I have ever seen is Hollywood. My dad was going to Iraq and he was stationed there in California. We went down on the dock and rode amazing rides, saw where Adam Sandler lived and visited a park named after him. We also went to Lego Land and saw a car made out of legos. We went to the San Diego Zoo. It was the biggest zoo I had ever seen. When it came time for my dad to leave I was really tired and I did not want him to go. He was gone for 11 months and now is back home. We are all happy he's home.

- The most amazing thing I have seen was my dog's luck. It was his birthday and we walked him to a lake nearby. The snow was melting and ducks swam on the melted side of the lake. My dad, my sister and I walked to a different side of the lake when it happened. My dog and the ducks fell into the freezing water, the ducks quacking as if they were laughing at him. He was trying to climb up onto the ice, not succeeding. By the time we got to him, he jumped onto the ice and looked like nothing had ever happened. And only a minute ago he was yelping in fright.

- The most amazing thing I have ever done would be when I was in New Jersey at my Aunt Nora's house, and I landed on my feet on a trampoline and I landed a front flip. That was a huge accomplishment for me! The front flip took two weeks to master.

- The most amazing place I have been is Hawaii because I always wanted to go there and when I finally did, it made me go WOW! They have huge waves that are very fun to ride on! They have very warm weather and soft sand. It is very sunny and it has a lot of fun things to do. I went horseback riding and it was the most fun I have ever had. Hawaii is an amazing place.

*I want to be a truck driver.*

- The most amazing place I've ever been was Ground Zero in New York City. I thought it was mind-blowing to know that those two gigantic structures once stood for more than twenty years but then came crashing down on top of the seven-level mall underneath the towers on that horrible day. It was also the saddest thing I have ever seen because I knew of all the people who lost their lives . . . . in the buildings and on the planes.

- The most amazing thing that happened to me was when I was face to face with a deer. When I was walking with my cousins we saw a big buck. As we walked towards it, it stood still, it didn't blink, and it just stood there. We stopped and were about five feet away from it. We thought it would have run away, but it walked towards us. I was frightened, but at the same time, it was amazing. This big deer walking towards us just made me say WOW out loud! When it was face to face to us it sniffed, turned around, and just walked away. That was the most amazing thing that happened to me.

- The most amazing thing I have ever seen is the Thousand Islands from a watch tower that is one half mile high. You can find this tower if you drive to Canada through the Thousand Islands. From this tower you can see every river, lake, and island that is a part of the Thousand Islands.

- Coney Island was great for me. The hot dogs and cheeseburgers were perfect there.

- The most amazing thing I ever saw was the fireworks on the 4$^{th}$ of July. They were awesome, loud, blasting, my chest was pounding. The sight of them, the color. I thought the earth was going to end.

- The most amazing thing I ever saw was the 2000-2001 school year's meteor shower. It was beautiful! It was so big that it looked like angels flying. Unfortunately, I had to stay up from midnight to 2:30 A.M. However, it was worth it. There were at least two meteors per second. That is the most amazing thing I have ever seen.

- I only have one favorite place. That place is home. I have my dog and cat which is my zoo. I can play with them and sleep with them. My backyard is my amusement park. The swings are a roller coaster. I can kick a ball or slide down my slide. I have my pool which is the ocean. The ripples in the water are huge waves and the tubes and rafts are fish and dolphins. My room is like a field I can go to so I could be alone. The stairs are a mountain that you have to climb. In my bathroom is the beach. I could take a bath for hours. You don't have to go far to find paradise.

*I want to be a surgeon.*

LeAnne Brogan

- The most amazing place is my grandma's yard because in the spring and summer I can swim, ride my bike in to the woods where the trail is, help plant vegetables in the garden, and play my flute on the deck. Also, in the winter I can go snowboarding down the hill, make a snow fort, have a snowball fight and go sledding. In the fall I help rake the leaves and then jump into them. This is what I do every time I go over to her house.

- The most amazing person is my mom. She helps me and my brothers and sisters with our homework. She cooks dinner every night. She does the dishes and laundry. She cleans the house. She drives us to activities such as baseball, dance lessons, cross country, track and marching band lessons. She works for the fire and ambulance company. She drives us to school. She is most amazing to me and she is the mother of nine.

- The most amazing person is Martin Luther King because he got the blacks and whites together. You have to have a lot of courage to stand up for what you believe in. If it wasn't for him then our world would be really depressing cause you would only be able to talk to your own color and no one else but your own color.

- I think firefighters are spectacular. I mean, many people like them because they think firefighters have a fun, exciting job. Working with fire is not fun or exciting. Once when I saw a fire, I shuttered just looking at it. Can you imagine how the people inside felt? Or how the firefighters felt? They have to be so brave. When I feel discouraged, I think about what they deal with. Firefighters have to leave their families and their children when called for an emergency. This is an extraordinary, dangerous job, but it is very helpful.

- The most amazing time and place I have ever been to would be my best friend, Megan's house on June 16, 2006. Her grandfather is the million dollar man of South Carolina. June 16th is her birthday and my birthday. They put my name on the birthday cake too, in purple and green, with flowers all around it. That made me feel good. We had gifts for each other so we could go shopping together. Then for 30 minutes we stayed in her room and sucked air out of helium balloons and started to sing. HAPPY BIRTHDAY! We had so much fun that day!

- The most amazing time was when I went hunting with my grandfather. I got to use his first gun. I passed my hunter safety course test and I'm a good shot. I aimed, took it off safety and shot. It was my first squirrel. I'm only 11, and I'm a girl. It was very great to go with him that day.

*I want to be the President.*

- The most amazing time was when I scored three goals in the championship soccer game and we won! We got trophies and had a pizza party!

- The most amazing thing that I am going to talk about is a person. When I went to Florida in March for spring training, I saw the Yankees play. Derek Jeter plays on the Yankees and I really admire and look up to him. During the National Anthem, I went over to the Yankees dugout and I yelled to Derek Jeter and I showed him my jersey and he signed it for me. He is the most amazing person I've ever seen.

- The most amazing thing that I have ever seen is JFK's Memorial grave because the flame never goes out and it is the most calming and soothing place that I have ever been to. The grave is placed in Washington D.C. Memorial Cemetery. As you know, JFK was an honorable president and his grave is amazing.

- The most amazing thing I have ever seen is the Statue of Liberty. I realize what it means because my great grandparents came over to the United States right from England. The Statue symbolizes freedom and it is very important to me. It also is amazing because it is a piece of history. It is very old and changed in color but still standing, still symbolizing freedom.

- The most amazing thing I've ever seen was watching a flip over in a NASCAR race on February 18, coming to the checkered flag and watching the big wreck at the same time, and watching Kevin Harvick and Mark Martin drag racing to the checkered flag at the same time and Kevin Harvick won by a fender at the Daytona 500 Race.

- The most amazing person I have ever seen was my Grandma Nancy. She was really fun. I always used to crawl in her hospital bed with her and watch TV. She was really sick and she couldn't have any candy and she had a stash of lollipops under her bed and we always used to eat them. One day she had to go to the hospital, but not for the lollipops. My aunt stayed with her every night. After two days, my grandma died. I miss her.

- The most amazing thing that happened to me was when my baby brother was born. I really wanted a sister. But I loved my new baby brother. I was so excited and happy. Even though I really wanted a baby sister, I love and am very happy to have a baby brother instead of a sister.

*I want to be a millionaire.*

- The most amazing place I have ever been to would be New York City. It was amazing because we got to see the Statue of Liberty, Times Square and Ground Zero. I loved being there. It was really crowded with lots and lots of people. There were tons of vendors everywhere and they weren't that expensive either. I also went to the giant Toys R Us. It has four floors. Most toys are for kids ten and under. There was a huge Ferris wheel too. We went to this really expensive restaurant. They wanted $30 just for a plate of spaghetti, and $300 for a glass of wine!

*I want to win on American Idol.*

# Chapter 10

**Writers of Eighth Grade share something that they love about their grandmother or grandfather**

- I love the way my grandmother is loving and doesn't yell like parents, and that she gives you what you want, and lots of goodies too.

- My grandma is special to me. She is my yai yai. (Greek for Grandma) She makes delicious food and buys me nice clothes. She makes me feel like a princess. My grandma loves me for who I am.

- I loved that my grandfather used to carry hard candy to make us feel better when we were little. He also gave us great gifts at Christmas.

- I love how my grandmother lives next door to me and calls me every day to see if I'm okay.

- My grandfather is 76 years old and he still gets his pool ready for all the grandkids. He also puts up all the Christmas decorations, just for the kids.

- I love my grandparents because whenever I go over their house, there is a big meal waiting for me. It always is delicious.

- Some reasons I like my grandfather are because he is full of life, especially at all of my basketball games. He is the loudest fan causing attention; just like

*I want to be a nurse who helps to deliver babies.*

my mother and me. He is fun to have around, but not always. He sometimes is grumpy, but usually is funny and outgoing. He always says I'm his favorite, but he likes us all equally. Those are some reasons I like my grandfather.

- I adore my grandmother for many reasons. One is her overwhelming kindness and generosity. Not to mention her superb baking skills. My grandfather is also very special to me. I value him because of his wisdom and ingenuity.

- All of my grandparents are gone. They lived in New York, so I couldn't visit them very often. My mom's parents died before I was born and my dad's parents died last year. One thing I remember and like, about my grandfather on my dad's side, was that he loved his Doberman pinscher, Ginger. My grandfather loved Dobermans and that's why we have one now. His name is Oscar.

- I love my grandpa because he yells at his tools when things don't go the right way.

- What I love about my grandmother is how she always talked to me in Italian and how she would eat meat right off of the bone. There would be no meat left and our dog Speckles wouldn't even want it.

- Because my Noni came from Italy, she always tells us stories from there, and always cooks pasta on Sundays. She sticks up for me and doesn't make me go to bed. I think she is religious because she lived in an orphanage in Italy after her parents died. I will always look up to her.

- My Nana lives nine hours away by car. But I feel like she is my next door neighbor. I love her for many reasons. She calls a lot and writes me letters. I appreciate how she makes a lot of her gifts she gives me for Christmas. I feel that my Nana is giving me a piece of her. I think I am extremely lucky to have a Nana like her. She knits, quilts, and bakes the best gingersnaps at Christmas time.

- My grandmother is very direct. If she wants something, she goes and gets it. If someone in the bank counts her money wrong or cheats my grandma off at the grocery store, she'll hunt them down and she will get it back. She's very close to her friends and wants us to have such a good time like she does. She tells me, "We can't waste any time while we're still young!"

- I call my grandmother "Nanny" and what I like most about her is that she is always there for me and I can open up to her and she would help me with

*I want to be a veterinarian.*

my troubles. I also like that she tells me family things that happened in the past. She is like my own personal therapist and I can tell her anything. She is great!

- What I love about my grandmother is she is such a strong person. It's been a little over a year since my grandfather passed away, and yes she is sad, and yes, she gets lonely, but she doesn't dwell on that fact. She wants to live the rest of her life the best way she can so she is staying strong and I love how she is able to do that.

- I love the smell of lasagna when I visit my grandparents. I know that Grammy's in the kitchen cooking. They know I love it! I smell woodchips too. I know that they are flying through the air and I can see my Pop Pop. Give him some wood, hammer and nails and he could build a house! There are so many things special about my grandparents, but the most special is how they share their love with the world.

- I miss my grandfather. He recently passed away. I used to go down in my basement with him and we'd watch cartoons and he'd let me take a sip of his beer. He would let me wear his favorite blue-lined hat. We used to play hide and seek with my grandmother too, who is the sweetest lady ever. She wouldn't hurt a fly. I miss my grandfather, but I know he is in a better place. Thank you.

- My grandfather takes me ice fishing in the winter time. I love my grandmother's funnel cakes.

- I love that I get to spend time with them whenever I want because some people don't get that opportunity.

- My grandmother makes the best French toast. I love her.

- My grandfather makes me bologna sandwiches.

- One thing I love about my grandmother is that when I was little she gave me a necklace. The necklace was a skull necklace. She knew I wanted it because I wanted to be a pirate for Halloween. I still have it and I will always love that skull necklace.

- My grandpa was old and could barely walk, but he was a funny old man. He used to take his teeth out and scare me and my brother when we were not looking.

*I want to be a cake decorator.*

- The best thing I like about my grandparents is that my grandfather tells me stories about when he was in the war. My grandmother takes me on walks in the woods and we collect flowers.

- I remember my grandmother very well. She was the greatest person ever. My grandmother had Alzheimer's disease but she would make me smile. She used to point her finger and say, "You're wonderful!"

- When some people think of the word grandparents, they think money or presents. When I think of grandparents I think love and kindness. I love them because they love me and care about them.

- One thing I really love about my grandpa was how he never gave up. He passed away six years ago, when I was only in second grade. He had a brain tumor. I saw the pain he went through. He never gave up even when times got rough. I hope I can be as strong as my grandpa.

- My grandfather always used to rock me in his lap and tickle me. He made the greatest, real mashed potatoes, and no one else could make them like him. (not even close) I miss him, but I'll always remember how great he was.

- I remember playing cards and dice with my Granny whenever we would go over her house. Sometimes, we would play poker and blackjack and use quarters.

- I love how my grandfather is always happy to see someone when they come to visit.

- There are so many things I admire my grandma for. She lived with eleven brothers and sisters and managed to work in factories for money for her family. She was strong and helped support her family after her father died of lung cancer. She is someone I'll always admire.

- I like my grandpa because he is funny, caring, kind, and he has an awesome beard.

*I want to be a game show host like Bob Barker.*

- My grandfather loved to read. He read the newspaper, every page. When he ran out of things to read, he even read my textbooks, the dictionary and then encyclopedias. He was the smartest man I know.

- My nana made the best homemade cinnamon and twisty buns. She would punch that raised dough; roll it out on a giant wooden cutting board; there would be flour everywhere! Cinnamon and sugar and her special hands forming the buns. I remember the smell of them baking in her house. It smelled and they tasted so good! She'd make enough for her card lady friends too.

- Nanny always had enough food to feed an army. "Better belly busted than good food wasted," she'd say.

- My Grandpap hunted and fished. We caught the biggest bass in Canada.

- My Grandpa lived at 37 Putnam Street. We used to make smores in the backyard with all of my cousins, Logan, Reagan, Shelby, Jilly and Jeff. One time Logan's marshmallow caught on fire. He ran around the yard yelling and screamin, "My mellows on fire!" Grandpa came to the rescue and blew it out.

- I love my grampa when he takes me to school. He doesn't give me kisses like Mom does in front of my friends.

- Me and my Zez won a look-a-like contest at the Funfest. We got our picture in the paper and a plaque and a free dinner for my whole family.

- My nanny's hooked on Atlantic City. She loves to play bingo and the slot machines. She gets this jingling look in her eyes when its time to go. I've been saving my quarters until I am old enough to go with her.

*I want to be a NBA player because I'm good at basketball.*

# Chapter 11

## One-liners and Briefs

"Is *whatever* a bad word?" Colin questioned.

"I wish today were yesterday," Mauro said.

"How can I get up so early and still be late?" Olivia sighed.

"Salutations," Katelyn welcomed.

"It's like a warm graveyard out there this morning," Cameron commented on the earthworms covering the macadam in the parking lot early one spring morning. Made me feel a bit squirmy.

Tyler seriously approached me by the school entrance, clutching his Star Wars stickers and said, "Mrs. Brogan, you must go to Boba Fett.com. It's the most awesome website about everything Star Wars! My dad and I were exploring it last night."

"Bah, bah, bah, but, I didn't do it," Brianna said. "J, J, J, Jesse did it first."

Carter, a kindergarten student in Mrs. Willis's class, asked her before the morning message, "Mrs. Willis, when are we going out for our cook-out, at lunchtime?"

"Why do they make us come to school when it's raining?" Connor asked his teacher as he approached her, squeaking his sneakers with every step.

*I want to be an inventor who invents new toys.*

After reading the book *Whales Passing* by Eve Bunting, a story about whales, to her kindergarten class, Rachel declared to the class, "My dog Peanut is fat like a whale and we still love her!"

"I forgot my homework again, and my book too," Julie said.
"Remind yourself to remember the next time," Mrs. Joseph said. "See if that works for you."

"My mom packed cucumbers in my lunch today," Robyn timidly said. "I just love cucumbers. I love celery with ranch dressing too."

We're moving to Tennessee, Walter announced in front of the class, because my mom likes country men, and there are no country men here.

"Hmmm," Tommy said to Miss Bonnie in the lunchroom, "This chicken patty tastes just like chicken."

The #1 rule in the library is "quiet." The most needed item in every classroom is tissues, because you just never know when you'll need them.

"My sisters are here today," Megan said to Terri, the security guard. "I wasn't here yesterday. My mom kept me home because I had pink eye or golden eye or something."

"I'm having a sleepover at my Memom's tomorrow night," Abby said to me as she walked through the school entryway. "We are going to watch *Curious George* on her new big screen TV."

After speech therapy with Miss Gin, Chris enjoyed a few minutes to chat with her about his summer vacation. He loved visiting the many water parks in the Pocono area. Chris asked Miss Gin if she had any kids and where did they go over the summer. She told him that she was a single woman and had no children. "Well," he said to her, "You should get some kids and go to Dorney Park!"

On another occasion, Miss Gin had a group of 4th grade students in her tiny classroom. Sometimes her students arrived before she came into her room. To her surprise, they'd sneak inside, turn the lights off, hide under her table and scare her when she opened the door.
"Things can get crazy, Miss Gin. It's just like raising children," Brendan, (one of the boys hiding under her table), said to her that day.

*I want to drive a FedEx truck.*

At breakfast one morning in the cafeteria, little Destiny meandered in, slid off her clear backpack and pink jacket, and walked up to get her tray for breakfast. On the way back to her seat she looked up at me with her elegant amber eyes, page boy haircut, grinned with a slightly mobile front tooth and said to me, "I just wuv Wucky Charms. I wuv buttered bread, and I wuv Santa too. I'm not afraid of him anymore. I'm too old to be afraid. I'm in first grade now, my Mommy said."

Michael looked wearisome over his shoulder at his enabler, Mr. Charlie. "Mr. Charlie," he whispered, "I feel pale."

Little Kathryn looked curiously at Mrs. Dolon as they walked hand-in-hand towards the girls bathroom. "Mrs. Dolon," she said, "How come your front side looks the same as your backside?"

"How can a farmer be a teacher?" Sandy asked her teacher, Mr. Berger.

He replied, "Just like a father can be a doctor, a carpenter can be an artist, a nurse can be a waitress.

Remember, I always tell my students, you can be anything you want to be or set your mind to be. What do you want to be when you grow up Sandy?"

I forgot to tell you, Mr. Young. Not only am I an asthmatic, I am lack toast and tolerant. (lactose intolerant)

"We are not having a potty-party right now," Mrs. Scott said to her fourth grade Social Studies class. When one is let free from the classroom, one by one by one by one, they all have to go.

Miss O'Brien's class formed into groups for guided reading time. She explained to her students what she expected them to do within their group as they read the story. Upon asking if everyone was ready to begin, Timothy Conahan cupped his hands over his mouth and shouted out loud, "Bring it on, Miss O.B.!"

Mrs. Hogan was practicing letter, number and picture recognition with young Samuel one morning in a quiet area by the reference section of the library. She showed him a picture of a fireplace. "What is this picture of Sam?" she asked him.

"Santa's hole," he replied.

"Mrs. Shulenski, can you move the diesel (easel) so that I can write on the board?" Billy asked.

*I want to work at the Mall.*

Carley was so excited to meet her second grade teacher, Mrs. Hauze, on the first day of school. She said, "I looked your picture up in the yearbook, and I have to tell you, Mrs. Hauze, you look so much better in person."

"I tooted on the field trip at the movies today," Rosella confided to her best friend Tanya. "Pooh stinky, wasn't it?"

"Yes, it was, Rosy," declared Tanya. "You knocked the entire row off their feet with that rip!"

"We put so much pressure on ourselves, and we enjoy doing it!" Mrs. Gallagher remarked.

Five fidgety first grade girls, lined up from left to right, Kcie, Kayla, Kristin, Allie, and Annie, stood with their backs toward me at the opposite end of the cafeteria. They seemed to be mesmerized by something. I could not imagine what they were peering at over the shiny stainless steel counter where the cafeteria ladies served lunch. Puppies in a pet store window, their curious concentration seemed to relate to. I began to walk toward them to see what their fascination was to appease myself.

Nancy, one of the head cafeteria women monitored a slicing machine, and then she walked away from it to begin making Italian hoagies that were on the menu for the day. An automatic slicing machine, slicing ham back and forth, back and forth, consistently and productively, had these five young ladies in a bit of a trance. I believe they thought it was a magical mystery machine, (you are becoming very, very sleepy) obviously hypnotized by its smooth, steady operation. I clapped my hands to break the silence. I was just in time before one of them dropped to the floor. "Girls, time for homeroom," I interrupted. Surprised by my presence and taken off guard, they did an about face and headed for the doorway. Ah, the simple pleasures of life that we are amused by!

Mrs. DeSpirito's son, Evan, played on the Valley East Little League team. One Saturday afternoon her youngest son, Kyle, who was staying with his grandparents for the day, called her on her cell phone. "Grandmom and Granddad want to take me to the movies," he said to his mother. "Can I go?" he asked. "Grammy," he hollered, "Mom's at Evan's baseball game working the confession stand, and she said it's O.K. with her!"

"My socks smell like snow," Elizabeth said.

Kayla, a 6$^{th}$ grader in Mrs. Steber's room, entered the school carrying five heavy textbooks, a designer Dooney and Bourke purse hanging from one

*I want to be a pilot and fly around the world.*

arm, and her lunch bag dangling from the other. "I was absent yesterday, Mrs. Brogan, and we had the gourmet coffee fund raiser pick-up. Where am I supposed to pick up my order? My dad's waiting outside in the car. He wanted me to find out."

"I'd have your dad pull around the front of the building, come in and ask the girls in the office," I replied. I'm not sure where you need to pick up your order."

"Oh, he can't do that Mrs. Brogan. He's in his pajama pants and he never has his boxers on."

Anthony sat next to his gifted teacher Mrs. Shelly in the library, early one Wednesday morning. He was reading *Horton Hears a Who,* by Dr. Seuss. "Who taught you how to read so well?" asked Mrs. Shelly.

"My mom teached me to read when I was four," he replied. "She teached my other brother too."

Ryan Wade is in the fourth grade. He talks consistently, rapidly and routinely, somewhat like an articulate antique auctioneer. Low-toned and persistent, everyone knows Ryan. His rounded face always has a smile, dark eyebrows and eyelashes against his ivory-colored skin, and Alvin the Chipmunk cheeks accent Ryan's special spunk.

One morning he walked alongside his teacher, Mrs. Ferrance, explaining to her in detail that today was Wednesday; he had his clarinet instrumental lesson with Mr. Boyle, and he wanted to be reminded of the time of his lesson before English class. He absolutely had to be prompt; after all they were practicing for the gala Spring Concert. He continued with his conversation making little or no eye contact with his teacher. Mrs. Ferrance tried to interrupt Ryan, tried to be polite, and tried to excuse herself to step into the faculty room for her morning coffee.

She turned to the right and entered the faculty room; Ryan continued to walk straightforward, continuing his conversation with her. He held his books in his left hand, his right hand constantly gesturing, as if she were right alongside him and his voice kept on chattering. A mere two minutes had passed; Mrs. Ferrance had her coffee in hand, caught up to Ryan and jumped into the conversation with him. "I assure you Ryan that you will be on time for your lesson today. Trust me."

"Oh, oh yes, yes, indeed, I trust you. Is it almost time for my lesson? Or the bell? Which is it?"

In November, Ms. Gilmore, library skills teacher, was talking to her 4th grade class about customs and traditions. "Let's have a raise of hands here class. How many of us have traditional turkey, stuffing, mashed potatoes, cranberry sauce and pumpkin pie for Thanksgiving?"

*I want to be an Avon Lady.*

All hands waved high into the air, except for Mitchell's. Ms. Gilmore turned toward Mitchell and asked what his tradition was.

"We always have something other than turkey," replied Mitchell.

"And why is that?" asked Ms. Gilmore in her soft and polite voice.

"Just because we hate turkey," Mitchell replied. "My mom, dad, brother, and me hate it. If my sister Sara wants turkey, she goes to my grandmother's house. We have roast beef, gravy, mashed potatoes and chicken fingers instead," he said honestly. "My mom does make a pumpkin pie for my dad." We have traditions and we have choices. A little of each creates balance.

"You could tell someone was at the juice bar today," Mr. Veet said to Miss Sharon as Elizio walked into his classroom, just off the library. Elizio, an ESL (English as a Second Language) student of Mr. Veet's, walked into his classroom wearing Adidas sneakers with black crew socks, shiny yellow silk shorts and a once white collared short-sleeved shirt. The grape juice stain was everywhere! He wasn't bothered by it. Hey, accidents happen.

"Mom thought she'd give my dog, Rebel, another chance in the car today," said Elvi Jo. "He still threw up in the back seat again."

Mrs. Passon read a story titled *Springtime Friends* to her first grade class. Afterwards, she asked her students if anyone had seen any signs of spring outside. "Have you seen any buds on the trees or robins in your garden?" she questioned.

Natalie shot her hand into the air like Michael Jordan shot a basketball in an NBA game. "In my backward," Natalie exclaimed, "I saw a yehyo flower today Mrs. Passon. I think it was a dandyyion or maybe a daffydill. I know it was yehyo."

"Thanks for sharing your story," with a smile, responded Mrs. Passon.

Maggie smiled her grandest smile and pointed to her missing front tooth and said, "I got 41cents and $3.00 from the tooth fairy!"

"There is definitely fungus among us," Marvin gestured.

Miss Gera asked her second grade class if they remembered what a synonym was from way back in first grade. Most of her students gazed at the ceiling searching for falling stars in bamboozle world. Jason raised his hand and replied to her, "I know what cinnamon is! It's brown powder for baking cookies, and its in Cinnamon Apple Jacks and Cinnamon Toast Crunch! I like Cinnamon Apple Jacks better, Miss Gera," he smiled.

*I want to work at the ticket booth at Dorney Park and ride the rides for free.*

"Boys and girls, listen carefully. Since our nation will be voting for our new President this November, here is our writing assignment for today," Mr. Gibson said to his fourth graders. "Write what you will wear to have dinner with the President."

Within a few minutes, Gretel Hancock walked slowly to her teacher's desk, head lowered to her chest, eyes peering over the top of her dark-rimmed glasses and whispered, "Mr. Gibson, I don't think my mom will let me go."

Ms. Olenick's first grade class was creating an "opposites book." After a few examples of up-down, off-on, slow-fast, Jamie raised her hand and implied, "How about this one, TV-DVD?"

Miss Coreva circulated the room while her students worked on a math worksheet. She stopped by Christian's desk, who looked a bit bewildered and thought he may need some help. Christian gazed up at her and muttered, "I love you, Miss Coreva."

When she responded to him that she cared about him too, he said to her, "I was just saying that to get your attention."

It was the first day back from the Christmas / New Year's break. After Bryan had his new library book checked out and replied with his polite "Thank you, Mrs. Brogan," he proceeded to tell me this. "Mrs. Brogan," he whispered to me, "Mickey Mouse called me on Christmas Day. He told me I was going to Disney over the Martin Luther King holiday weekend. I was so excited about the call! I couldn't wait to tell you. I can't wait to get there. It's only 10 more days. My mom, dad, and my sister Alyssa and me are going to Disney on an airplane. That was the best Christmas present I could ever remember."

Justin, a seventh grade student, raised his hand during sustained silent reading and asked his teacher if he could go to see the nurse. "I have growing pains," he said, "and my knee hurts really bad."

"I woke up this morning with a great pain in my neck," Madeline said to her best friend Sophia. "I remember muttering out loud still half asleep, it's O.K. There is the tin man. He'll squirt a little oil in my neck from his silvery tin can. That'll do the trick! Then I woke up and my neck didn't hurt. Isn't that strange?"

Brandon, a kindergartener, said to his teacher the day before Christmas break, "Did I mention Santa was born out of a turkey?"

I love to see Lynn, Robert's mom, every Friday, as she kisses him off to school. Her final words to me are, "Have a good week-end!" I wait for those words every week.

*I want to be a jockey.*

# Chapter 12

## Acronyms

Here we go with acronyms.
Definition: a word made from the initial letters of a term or phrase.

*B.T.S.*—Back to school.
*M.Y.O.B.*—Mind your own business.
*B.T.*—Big trouble or *B.B.T.*—Big Big trouble. (There is always a big "whoooo hoooo!" when I use this one.)
*T.B.S.S.*—Too bad so sad.
*N.N.*—Not nice.
*N.C.*—No cutting!
*S.K.*—Super kid.
*S.D.K.*—Super duper kid.
*G.D.*—Good day.
*H.A.G.D.*—Have a good day.
*O.M.F.*—Owe me five. (Minutes at recess . . . they get it)
*N.H.*—No homework. (kids like to hear this one)
*H.P.*—Homework pass. (kids will pay other kids for these)
*T.G.I.F.*—Thank "goodness" it's Friday. (Everyone loves this one)
*T.T.Y.L.*—Talk to ya later.
*T.T.F.N.*—Ta ta for now.
*S.Y.T.*—See you tomorrow.
*N.P.*—No problem.
*T.Y.*—Thank you.
*P.P.S.*—Post P.S.S.A. syndrome
*Y.W.*—You're welcome.
*R.O.F.L.*—Rolling on floor laughing.

*I.D.K.*—I don't know.
*I.D.C.*—I don't care.
*T.Q.B.*—The Queen bee.
*B.B.*—Best behavior
*J.K.*—Just kidding.
*N.F.*—Not funny.
*B.M.I.*—Boost my identity.
*K.I.D.S.*—Kind, intelligent, dynamic schoolchildren.
*E.I.*—End It or *T.E.*—The End

*Add Your Own Here:*

_____
_____
_____
_____
_____
_____
_____

## Chapter 13

### Kids' Homework Excuses

You know that old saying, "I've heard every excuse in the book." "Well, no you haven't." When asking a student, "Where's your homework?" here are a few prize winning answers.

The initial questioning look from the guilty party is that peculiarly cringed-looking face, one eye squinting, one eyebrow raised, one corner of the mouth in a slight corkscrew curve, lips tight, not quite ready or willing to respond to the interrogation. A raspy voice emerges, slightly slurred, slightly stuttering:

1. "I told my mom what to do, but she didn't do it for me."
2. "Well, my dad took it to work. Can I go call him to find out if he's done with it?"
3. "My brother threw up on it."
4. "I mean, my brother and my sister threw up on it."
5. "My new puppy peed on it."
6. "Oh, we had to go shopping. No time."(This excuse came on a Monday.)
7. "My brother ate it on purpose. He has this 'thing' for paper."
8. "Homework? What homework? Did we have homework?"
9. "I have short term memory loss."
10. "It's at home. I did it. Was I supposed to bring it back?"
11. "My mom threw it out."
12. "We had a fire."
13. "My father was using our new shredder. It was on sale at Wal-Mart. I think he got carried away."
14. "I seriously did it, but it disappeared . . . honest."
15. "I swear I did it; (please, no swearing) maybe it's in my locker. Can I go look?"

16. "I didn't have any time. I had a game."
17. And here's a good one . . . "I did it . . . it was in my backpack, someone broke into our house and stole it."
18. My dad said do it in school . . . that's the teacher's job.
19. "Was I supposed to read the book for the book report? I'll never have it ready for today."
20. "I lost it. I sincerely lost it."
21. Enough said; end of excuses. Just do your homework!

# Chapter 14

**Parents' Excuses:
Calling their kids off from school**

School offices, primary, intermediate, secondary and administrative look and sound like the New York Stock Exchange on a major trade day in the morning. With the office personnel, faculty and staff signing-in, maintenance calls, security issues, approaching armies of buses, parents, late students, sick students, U.S. mail, UPS and FedEx pick-up and delivery, administrative meetings, conferences, coffee brewing, donuts ruling, and the unrelenting ring of the office telephones, the atmosphere can oftentimes be labeled as elevated, hustling, bustling, never a dull moment, typical harried morning routine. One senses the entity of the Tasmanian Devil spiraling from start to finish through the main office area. No Starbucks coffee or High Energy drinks needed here.

I give a "three cheers" and a "standing ovation" to the tireless women who keep structure, consistency, harmony and composure in the school offices every day. The telephones are ringing. Here are samples of what the caller has to say today and samples of what is written on notes sent into the office:

1. Jessie won't be in to school today. He was up all night with the poops.
2. Brendan's been blowing green from his nose since Friday. He won't be in today, or even tomorrow.
3. Evan's tonsils are the size of meatballs. We have to get to the doctor today. Could we get his homework, please?
4. Sorry, Joanne, Isabella won't be in today. We were up late last night watching a movie.
5. I absolutely can't send my kids in TODAY. The date is 06/06/06. We are a very superstitutious family. We won't be going outside today either.

6. We heard that it was going to snow today. I don't drive in bad weather.
7. Oh my gosh! The storm tracker just came across my TV screen! It's goin' to rain heavy at times today, and with nickel size hail! I can't bring the kids out in that!
8. Will there be an early dismissal today due to the wind factor?
9. Roger and Randy won't be in today. The premier of *The Simpson's* opens in theatre across the country today. We are going to get in line for the 1:00 matinee! We're getting ready now.
10. Martin won't get out of bed. He said he hates school and he's not going. We have to see his therapist.
11. They said his throat is stripped. I can't see any marks. And he can't come back for three days. I'll call back in three days.
12. Lice. All over. Samantha can't take swim class. Can she still come in for the Halloween party this afternoon?
13. Chicken pox, shall I send Josephina anyway, just so the other kids can get'em too?
14. Hi! I'm so sorry. We slept in again.
15. Sharon said there is going to be a fire drill today. Oh, that fire alarm really hurts her ears. Do you think it's OK to come in after the drill? Will you call me at 555-9876?
16. Mrs. Hancock said that the doctor said, "Everything's infected on Jeremy. Keep him home all week." "How will I get out for my weekly manicure?" she cried. "Will I need a doctor's excuse to bring him back?"
17. Please excuse Linda for being absent on January 10th. She was sick and I had to get her shot, twice.
18. Martin walked into the school office, stared at Joann working at her desk and light-headedly stated, "I feel unconscious." Knowing Martin's resistance to coming to school, Joann gingerly said to him, "Walk right through to the nurse's station, Martin, and lie down for a bit. You'll be just fine for your first period Pre Algebra class." (Can't put anything past the finely focused office staff)
19. Dear Principal, Please excuse Rebecca from school on February 28, 29, and 30.
20. My brother forgot to wake me up.
21. Kindly excuse Ronald from school yesterday. He fell out of our tree and broke his lips.
22. Mandy won't come in today. She's waiting for the tooth fairy to arrive.
23. Leslie won't be at school today. She has been sharting all night.
24. Jimmy was absent yesterday. Please excuse him. He had the diarrhea and his sneakers leak.
25. We forgot to change the clocks. Sharon won't be ready. Thank you.

26. Scott won't come in today. His nose is snotty and he can't take it when the kids call him Snotty Scotty.
27. Jessie, Jamie, Jonathan and Jerry won't be in. We're moving. Au revoir.
28. Annie was absent December 1$^{st}$, 2$^{nd}$, and 3$^{rd}$. She had a fever, sore throat, hives, and a headache. Her brother Kyle was absent December 3$^{rd}$, 4$^{th}$, and 5$^{th}$. He had body aches and a low grade fever. His stepsister, Marianna had two teeth break in overnight and everybody was fussy. I wasn't so great either, and their father was out of town on business.
29. A concerned parent calls the first day of school and asks the secretary, "Is there school the whole day today?"
30. A question arises about orientation. "Do I have to bring my child?" A day before school concern: When is the Halloween parade?
31. The mother of an 8$^{th}$ grade boy called and said that Jeremy was not in school today (Wednesday) because he was having a nervous breakdown. She said that she called the doctor, but the doctor could not get him in to see him until Friday, so he will be in school on Thursday and Friday morning, and she would pick him up early on Friday for the appointment.
32. Alyssa and Josh cannot make it to school today, Rita. Our dog got skunked, and we all smell.
33. Richard will not be at school today. He just lost all of his marbles.

# From a Teacher's Point of View

Mrs. Reynolds had a listening activity lesson planned on the technique of learning and following directions for her first grade class. She began to instruct her students with a series of commands. "Class, first clap your hands two times," she said. "Pause. Second, stamp your feet three times. Pause. Third, raise your hands high into the air," she instructed her students. "STOP." She repeated the basic directions two more times in front of the room, next to her neat and orderly desk.

"This time, you try it," she said.

The children were eager and ready and followed her lead exactly. They clapped two times. CLAP, CLAP. "Paws." Yes, you guessed it. The class then showed their clenched fists with arms outstretched, making their paws visible to Mrs. Reynolds. She instructed the class to continue. They stamped loudly, again raising their paws to her. Lastly, their paws shot straight into the air.

"Stop," recited Mrs. Reynolds. She paused. "Now, class, put your hands by your sides. You did an excellent job." Tomorrow's lesson, she thought to herself with a chuckle, is synonyms. Kids give such a kick, such a lift, catch a glimpse every chance you can.

Why did Nicholas so love the book, "*Dinosaur, Dinosaur?*" Week after week, Nicky, a second grade student, insisted upon borrowing the same book from the library. "It's a picture book, Nicholas, his teacher Mrs. Johnson said to him. "You are such an excellent reader. Why not try something to read with a bit more of a challenge? Let's take a look at the *Magic Tree House* series."

Nicholas, reluctantly put the book back on the book cart, with a sorrowful and somewhat discouraged look. "My mom always read this book to me," he said to his teacher. "She'd make up a new story every time. She liked dinosaurs as much as I do. It was the last book my mother read to me," his lower lip quivering. "Then she got sick, and she died."

Nicholas was seven. The dinosaur picture book undoubtedly made a great impression on him. He felt his mother's presence; he remembered his mother's voice.

"Let's see if we can order a copy from the book club, Nicky," his teacher said." I remember that it was available in last month's Scholastic pamphlet." He timidly smiled and chose another book.

"Thank you, Mrs. Johnson," he whispered.

Teachers make lasting impressions, build character, grant confidence, and affect a child's life. We all can make a difference. Here's a hug for all of the Nicholas's out there.

Everybody knows our one-of-a-kind maintenance man, A.J. A.J. stands around 5'5" tall, is lean as a palm tree, and has black hair with matching mustache and goatee. He always wears his favorite team sweatshirt and a baseball cap, the Philadelphia Eagles, or sometimes changes to his hunting and fishing favorite, Cabela's. His gait is rather sluggish, with his head lowered gazing at his feet or perhaps he's checking for black heel marks on the floor. I almost forgot he has a very distinct whistle. You just know when A.J.'s coming around the corner.

Mrs. King's kindergarten class headed towards Miss Flower's room for Art, caught sight of A.J. She shouted out, "Kindergarten, let's say hi to AJ."

"Hi A.J.," they'd all shout.

"Hi ya, kids," A.J. would respond.

Along with A.J., Vince and Mark round out the dayshift maintenance trio.

I recall the first day back to school late in August last year. I saw A.J. heading toward the library. He was on a mission in search of boxes of textbooks to deliver to our teachers on the second floor. "Nice to see you A.J.," I said.

"You too, LeAnne" was his response.

There was something a little different about him. Ah, his hair! He really had a few inches cropped off. "AJ, you got a haircut." I commented.

"I did indeed. Locks of Love," he replied.

"Locks of Love?" I questioned.

"Yeah, it's a non-profit organization that makes hairpieces for kids who lose their hair from cancer or some other disease. This is the second time I donated my hair, LeAnne. My mother Ruth has leukemia and she is in remission right now. I like to think that I'm helping in some way," he said. "Well, I better get these books upstairs, teachers are waiting. See ya later."

"See ya, A.J.," I said back to him.

Many school districts around the country provide meals to children during the summer months at local schools, parks, playgrounds and community centers. Ms. Walters, a food service coordinator from The National School Breakfast and Lunch Program, visited a locality one balmy summer day in July.

A small, four-year-old girl came in line to receive a meal. She was with an older sibling and was wearing worn-out red plaid, flannel feety pajamas. The elastic, rubbery sole on her left foot flapped against her heel as she walked. She patiently waited her turn, picked up a styrofoam tray, plastic utensils and a pint of chocolate milk. Ms. Walters's eyes were fixated on this child as she asked the youngster, "Would you like ham and cheese, turkey and cheese, or a peanut butter and jelly sandwich?"

"Peanut butter and jelly, please," she answered, with a beaming smile.

"Would you like a piece of fruit?" Ms. Walters's next question was.

"I can have fruit too?" the little girl responded in surprise.

"Yes, you may," replied Ms. Walters. "You are a growing young girl, just like those beautiful flowers over there," as Ms. Walters gestured toward a garden filled with wildflowers.

The young child gave Ms. Walters the biggest, warmest smile as she accepted the meal and she seemed so genuinely grateful. Ms. Walters was so touched by the look on her face. It made her realize how important it is to take advantage of all the programs offered in this country for children and make sure as adults we are doing everything we can to keep our children safe, fed, and educated.

March Madness is here! It is the month of the 3$^{rd}$ grade mammoth, out-of-this-world, annual gushing volcano assignment. Mindy remembered when her older brother Mason was in the third grade. She was only five-years-old at the time and in Miss Hinkle's kindergarten class. For some odd reason, thoughts of Easter flooded her mind when she thought about the time of the volcanoes in school. Maybe she had been dreaming. She had her big chance this year.

As the children studied about volcanoes at Mt. St. Helens, Washington, and Mt. Vesuvius, Italy, every third grade student in Mr.Bently's room was required to write a report, construct a model volcano, and on a very special and eventful day before the beginning of spring, had the opportunity to erupt their very own volcano in the classroom. The kids built their projects at home, out of Play-Dough, clay, papier mache, pebbles, stones, cardboard, or combinations of these materials, and then transported their creations to the school classroom to be displayed. Volcanoes ranged from a mere six inches tall to a monumental 66 inches tall, weighing ten ounces to ten pounds, shaped to perfection resembling giant Jell-O molds, moss covered tree stumps, and tornado twisted cylinders.

Every student (with parental supervision) designed their unique creation. When the day of eruption was designated, the students brought into school every bit of baking soda, vinegar, and red food coloring available to mankind. This combination of fine ingredients, placed strategically into the center of each volcanic beauty, created the ultimate frothy, foamy, and fizzling, flare-up on the first floor of the elementary school building! Among the shouts and screams, excited "oohs" and "aahs", the kids decided which volcano was awarded the "Best in Show."

That familiar smell of Easter flooded Mindy's mind that day when the volcano eruptions began. Gosh, she thought, Easter was four weeks away. Why was the smell of Easter eggs all over the school? She put on her thinking cap and tried to remember. She overheard her classmates demanding, "Put in lots of vinegar," as Chris instructed Carl. "I want my volcano to blast-off like the Fourth of July fireworks and the NASA Space Shuttle!" he bellowed.

"Quick, get another bottle!" Mark instructed.

"Slowly, pour it very slowly," Carl beckoned.

The light bulb began to blink on the top of Mindy's head like a police car chasing down a traffic violator. "Jiminy Crickets, that's it!" Mindy said to herself. "Vinegar. Add two tablespoons of household vinegar to the egg dye tablet, Mason," she recalled her mother's saying. All the colored cups, red, yellow, green, violet, orange and blue lined up on the kitchen table, ready to dip Mom's hard-boiled Easter eggs. That was it! Mystery solved. Vinegar and volcanoes= springtime and Easter. Vinegar, vinegar, add and smell the vinegar.

Mr. Carlton (an elementary gym teacher) was just about to walk out of the school office after receiving a telephone message, when his next kindergarten class came around the corner and down the hallway toward him. The line leader for that particular day, Jacqueline, saw Mr. Carlton and asked him if he was teaching their class gym that day. He replied to her, "Jacqueline, today you are going to have the nicest, richest, handsomest, most intelligent gym teacher ever!"

The young girl with big brown-eyed susan, button eyes looked at him with a terribly sad look on her face and replied, "No thanks, Mr. Carlton. We want you." Honestly, a true story.

Mrs. Larson taught at the prestigious St. Joseph's Catholic School for ten years before enrollment began to decline and the school was unfortunately forced to close. The principal, Monsignor Albright, was a solemn believer that the teachers and students should never pass an opportunity to attend mass, which naturally meant daily mass was mandatory. The school was situated on one side of the street, the church on the opposite side. A few nuns kept their residency within the school and were always available to help the children cross safely to the daily masses. The entire school would parade, two by two, led by Sister Mary Frances and Sister Geraldine, across the street to the church, and row by row seat themselves within the polished solid oak pews.

The children attended all types of masses and on one particular Friday morning there was a funeral mass, well attended by the community. After the congregation was seated, the organist began to play and the choir bellowed out with *Amazing Grace*. Father Albright began the mass and the casket was walked in from the rear of the church. It then proceeded up the aisle and stopped in front of the altar. The music subsided and the entire church was very quiet, solemn and serene. Mrs. Larson's class occupied the first two pews of the church. Suddenly, Jimmy Martin, a curious and assertive student in her class shouted out, "Hey, Mrs. Larson! What's in the box?"

The parishioners' eyes widened in disbelief and they clasped their wide open mouths in astonishment! Sobs of sorrow went silent as all eyes were fixated on Mrs. Larson and young Jimmy. Needless to say, Mrs. Larson's class never attended another funeral mass. True story.

Michael Fender, another young lad from St. Joseph's School, was preparing for the Sacrament of First Holy Communion. Sister Philomena and Sister Mary Margaret were teaching the children prayers and practicing for the church procession and celebration that would take place in early May. Bishop John from the Diocese of Scranton would be leading the procession and performing the ceremony, and they wanted the children to be prepared to do their very best. Michael oftentimes had difficulty concentrating and tended to fidget, pulling and tugging at his uniform pants, rolling and unraveling his tie until it resembled rumpled clothes in a dirty hamper. He unconsciously would make a clicking noise with his tongue, in his desperate desire to keep his body in motion.

On a frosty, flurrying mid-February day, Michael was experiencing an unusually "good" day. Sister Philomena asked him what the special occasion was that granted him such a wonderful change in his behavior. She and Sister Mary Margaret complimented him several times and told him how proud they were of him. Looking up at the ceiling of the church, stained glass saintly figures displaying all the holiness of the moment, with his index finger pointed, he knelt down and blurted, "God made me do it!"

The Sisters immediately fell to their knees, blessed themselves, clasped their rosaries, raised their heads with Michael, sighed, smiled and thanked the Good Lord for His Blessing.

Breakfast is offered to the students every morning before school begins. A lingering group of girls, I call them the "Breakfast Club" kids are religiously present, occupying the same table for their morning discussion about the previous nights events: who got booted from *American Idol*, who got tickets to see Hannah Montana, did Nathanial really ask Alyssa out? Gossip and rumors, hearsay and happenings were all the morning buzz. Words were uttered more than food was eaten. They are a bubbly, giddy bunch.

Mrs. Hudock, the meticulous cafeteria monitor, had the assignment of keeping these girls on their toes, an eyeful watch to the black and white circular wall clock, making certain they were trashing their trays by 8:55 A.M. As she scanned the lunchroom for possible spills, blown out straw papers, and foods about to be wasted, she passed by an unfamiliar face at the opposite side of the cafeteria. "Good morning," she said to a bright-eyed, fair haired smiling six-year old girl. "Welcome to our school," Mrs. Hudock continued. "And may I ask your name, this fine day?"

The little girl, with a mouthful of Corn Flakes answered, "Valerie."(Mrs. Hudock handed her a napkin)

"That is a very pretty name, Valerie," she replied.

"Yeah, my mom gave it to me when I was little," she said. What a sweet tart!

Checking the time, with a quick glance at the Breakfast Club and the wall clock, Mrs. Hudock flicked the lights off and on, signaling the girls to get a move on. The girls instantly got to their feet, shoved the last morsels of breakfast into their mouths, emptied their trays, picked up their belongings and marched off to class, still chattering. Valerie was right behind them. "Keep walking Little Miss Valerie. Don't want to be marked absent." Alas, kitchen's closed until 8:30 tomorrow morning!

Every morning, Mrs. Smith walks her three daughters, hand in hand in hand, to the school entrance and in through the corridor. Off walks Natasha, flaming red hair bouncing. Next goes Adriana, always a bit reluctant and in need of a gentle pushhhhh, after her kiss from mom, of course. The last of the three, is Daniella. Mrs. Smith always unzips her jacket, asks her if she wants a kiss, and checks to see that everything is in place.

One morning, Danielle had a smidge of jelly, or icing, or crust or some tidbit from breakfast on the corner of her mouth. Immediately her mother licked her very own motherly loving thumb, slightly stretched Danielle's cheek about as far as my "ON" switch on my laptop, and gently rubbed the smidge clean off the corner of her mouth with her thumb. I remember my mother performing that very identical gesture on me, when I was a kid. Do you? A little spit does the trick. A mother's finishing touch, just too special.

Ah, it was Merry Christmastime at the North Pocono School. This question always comes to my mind. "What do the hundreds and thousands of teachers do with the countless quantities of well-intentioned holiday gifts that practically every student in the classroom gives to each and every teacher year after year after year?" I guess that's something that I need to take the time to research.

Anyway, the last day before the Christmas break, in the midst of the holiday class parties, with orange drink and delicately decorated cupcakes, cold pizza and cheese curls, Mrs. Kelly sat at her desk opening the gifts, one by one, from her class. She tactfully opened a package from Marcus, with glistening red and gold wrapping paper and carefully lifted the lid of the satiny box. Inside the box was a glittery sapphire blue and white snowflake ornament, which appeared to be an expensive gift. (It was from the Dollar General. The price tag was still on it.) This truly was a child's idea of beautiful. Mrs. Kelly expressed great appreciation and thanked Marcus for his thoughtfulness and for the lovely gift.

Suddenly, Jason Fritz piped up in a very disappointed tone, "I wanted to get you that, Mrs. Kelly, but my mom said I had to get something cheap." Ah, the joys of the season. Happy Holidays! (By the way, I think Dollar Store items rock!)

Travis, a kindergarten student in Mrs. Currey's class, hesitantly handed a note to his teacher that his mother had written early that morning. This is what the note read,

> Dear Mrs. Currey,
> Please excuse Travis from classes today at 1:30 P.M. He has a dental appointment with Dr. Barna. He has a bad tooth. His toothbrush is in his Spiderman lunch box. Can you have him brush his teeth after lunch in the boy's room? Make sure he has his homework because he will forget it anyway. Thank you very much.
> Mrs. Jones

Mrs. Currey had Rita in the office call her room at 1:10 that afternoon, and Travis and his lunchbox, and his homework paper in his blue folder, and his Yankees baseball cap, strutted to the office to wait for his mother. The next day, Mrs. Currey asked Travis how everything went at the dentist. Travis replied, "My bad tooth had an 'absence' (abscess) and that was why I missed school and why I had to go to the dentist! He gave me some pink Bionic (anti-biotic) medicine to take, like the Power Rangers do to make them strong. I feel pretty mighty today, and my toothache went away."

"That's wonderful news," replied Mrs. Currey. "I am glad you are feeling better."

Concerned ten year-old Anthony characteristically expelled his distinctive sneeze, wiped his nose with a Kleenex, and said to his teacher, "Mrs. Rusk, ever since I was a little kid, everybody in my house, in my church, in the mall or wherever I might be stops and stares at me after I sneeze."

When Anthony sneezed, it sounded similar to a large piece of heavy equipment crunching the hood of a junker car. "I can't control the sound or the after splash any more than a horse flicks his tail to fend off flies. Everyone's eyes always look as though they are about to pop out of their sockets, mouths dropping wide open and they look at me really funny, making me feel very uncomfortable."

"You do have a rather unique and unusual sneeze, Anthony," Mrs. Rusk relayed to him. "Do you think it's possible you could try and sneeze a little more softly or quietly or simply remember to cup your hands over your face?"

"I don't know, I never really thought about it, Mrs. Rusk. It's my natural way of sneezing, Mrs. Rusk. I guess I could try." He went on, "I just don't know what I'll sound like when I become a man. Will I stop traffic? Will I cause an accident? Or worse, will I give somebody a heart attack? That's what really worries me," he said.

"Anthony," Mrs. Rusk replied with understanding and compassion, "Don't worry about what the future will bring. You just might outgrow it." Your sneeze is uniquely you.

It's Friday! TGIF and kindergarten *Show and Tell* day! The letter of the week was the letter *B*. Jessica brought in her favorite overstuffed bunny, Blister. There were beach balls, baseballs, balloons, barrettes, Barbies, binoculars and Band-Aids just to name a few.

As the children brought out their show and tell items, quick as lightning, Olivia snatched Jessica's bunny, Blister, and stuffed him into her purple plaid Capri pants! With the class in a mild uproar, their teacher, Mrs. Simmons, knew exactly where she needed to send little Miss Olivia. This was a job for the school nurse. A volunteer mother in the classroom for the morning took Olivia's hand and headed for Mrs. Stefan's office. She was responsible for the proper procedure and protocol, and used her expertise in restoring Blister to the classroom for *Show and Tell*. Every school nurse has her daily challenges, of all kinds!" Hip, hip, Hooray, I say, to all of our school nurses!"

Maintenance manager Mark installed two foam hand dispensing sanitizers on either side of the cafeteria one Monday morning before the lunchtime bell. "What a great idea!" I thought, "another way to combat those sickening germs that travel throughout the school." The white foamy hand sanitizer spurted out just the right amount when you placed your hands directly underneath the unit. It was not necessary to touch it, fingerprint it, or contaminate it.

There turned out to be one minute problem with this device. Perfect it was for disinfecting the tiny hands of kindergarten through the middle school age students. It was also placed at the perfect height of the smaller children's heads as they walked into the lunch line. Because they were just the right size, a number of students walked underneath the dispensing unit. I began to see a few white frothy splotches appear on the students' heads at that noteworthy 11:55 A.M. lunch period. Lunchroom monitors, I think it's time to redirect the students' pathway to line up for their meals.

Several of Mrs. Flanagan's students were waiting good-naturedly in her classroom for their bus to be called at the end of the day. They were talking about one of their favorite teachers, Mr. Hanson, who had retired the previous year. Alexis Hancock asked Mrs. Flanagan when she was going to retire. She laughed and said, "Not for a long time, unless I win the lottery." The young girl asked what she meant by that remark. Mrs. Flanagan informed the class that if she won the lottery, then she wouldn't need the money she made from teaching.

Another of the students said to her in amazement, "You mean you get paid to do this?"

One day after lunch, Ms. Ferry was walking her students back to the classroom from the cafeteria. As they passed the faculty room, they observed a few of the teachers leaving to meet their own classes. One of her students, Joseph Evans asked, "Ms. Ferry, do you know what I am going to be when I grow up?"

"No, I don't," she replied, "What do you want to be?"

He said, "When I finish school, I am going to go to college and then come back and be a teacher right here in this school."

"That is a great plan," Ms. Ferry said to Joseph.

He then asked her if she knew why he wanted to do that. She was expecting an answer along the lines of wanting to help children. His answer was, "Because then I can go into the teachers' room and get a snack out of the machine," he replied.

March 31st through April 3rd was the week set aside for PSSA (Pennsylvania System of School Assessment) testing from grades 3-8. Principal Peters had announced every morning for a week prior to the testing how important it was for the students to get a good night's rest, eat a good breakfast, be a good listener, keep focused and on task, and to always try their best. Any student who needed additional time to complete his test or those who were absent on any of the testing days, would be escorted to the library. It was an abnormally quiet atmosphere inside the school. The sound, or lack of it, reminded me of a waiting room in a doctor's office, or as though a real lockdown were in effect, one of the many drills we practice with the students throughout the year.

Paula and I were the designated runners for the week, transporting the crated test booklets from each classroom down the elevator into the guidance office. On one drive-by into the office, I pulled my test "pick-up trolley" towards the half swinging door and heard the women in the office laughing out loud. The nurse, our two secretaries, gym teacher, 8th grade science teacher and a student teacher were all in the office. I noticed that the television was on. I glanced at the screen to see what was so funny; however, the news was on, and the scene was not at all humorous. Then I heard a cheer, and I looked toward the women.

Student teacher, Ms. Staruch stood erect holding steady a hand-made paper airplane in her hand. She had her eyes focused and ready to take aim at the teachers' cubicle mailboxes which were adjacent to the office countertop. She was trying to get her airplane in for the score. She let it fly and sure enough it landed right inside Mr. Penkala's mailbox slot. The office crowd laughed and cheered! Next up, was Miss Turri. Her plane made a beeline to the right, glided through the office doorway and landed safely in the hall. Now it was my turn. I released my right hand from my trolley, took hold of the paper airplane, positioned myself behind the counter, took aim and fired. It shot upward like a hot air balloon, just grazing the ceiling, and landed on top of a spider plant setting on the top of the mailboxes. The timing was just right to catch the women in the office "off duty" for a few minutes.

Mrs. Cannon's class was enjoying a special activity as a reward for good behavior. It was a pizza and movie afternoon. Several students were not able to participate due to behavior problems. The students who were out of the activity were asked to write about why they were not able to participate and what they would do differently so that they could attend the next special activity. Brittany, a lively conversationalist realized her problem and came up with a unique plan to help. She wrote that the reason that she missed the activity was because "I talk too much and call out anytime I want to and then my class can't learn." Her solution was "I need to stop talking and calling out in class, so I will pretend that I can't speak English."

Mrs. Mackay is a Special Education Resource Room teacher at Parks Elementary School. She has a very distinct relationship with her one and only Spanish student, Julio. She calls him "Julio Dear." One afternoon, Julio said to Mrs. Mackay, "I'm no deer, I like horses. I'm Julio Horse." Sometimes, he'll substitute another animal for horse, like seal, or tiger, or jaguar. "But never deer," he says, because he just don't like deer!

"Bye Dillon," Nadine waved.
"Be seein' ya."
"Bye Dillon, be a good boy," said Miss Evancho as she shook his hand, then gave him a hug. Six-year-old Dillon came from a family of four. Mom left him and his siblings with Grandfather to raise them. Grandfather gave them to a reputable Social Services Agency to place the children in foster homes.

The first home took Dillon in for three weeks. His siblings were all placed in separate locations. Dillon came to school on a bus and walked into the cafeteria each morning for breakfast. He usually procrastinated until the bell rang and I would skedaddle him off to class. After three short weeks, he was placed in a new home. This loving family had one natural daughter, Maria, age three. The

Tancin's drove Dillon to school in their Dodge Caravan every day. He came into school early one morning in March, grinning from ear to ear and said to me, "Mrs. Brogan, I don't have to come in for breakfast in the cafeteria any more. The house I'm in now has breakfast in the morning for me." He started to wear his glasses and made a few friends.

Four weeks went by. We could see that he was becoming comfortable with his new family, his surroundings and his school, and trusting the adults that he came in contact with each day: his teachers, school aides, the lunch ladies, the janitors, and the girls in the office. He seemed happier. March went out like a lion. The lion carried Dillon away to another foster home in another school district. We miss you, Dillon, we all miss you. I pray for Dillon and all the other foster children who await good homes in our country.

While reviewing math facts with his second grade class, Mr. Grant included a game of math Bingo. Kids love a classic, old-fashioned game and can have fun while learning. What a neat idea!

A calm and cool-headed, crew-cut Kenneth, obviously hoping for a reaction from his class, stood up and asked, "Does anyone feel like they're at an Old People Bingo?" Kenny had a very unique, quirky monotone to his voice. He was a difficult child to get a smile from too. He went on, "My Nana rules at BINGO! She plays every day at the Old Peoples Center. My Nana can play thirty cards at one time, and some of her gambling friends do too! They're like wide-eyed sorcerers! Every one of 'em has these trays of colored Bingo wands, all the colors of the rainbow. They dab those colors on those Bingo cards faster than I can get a math problem done. You should see 'em! They work like Speedy Gonzales and the Road Runner!"

Mr. Grant and the entire class laughed out loud. "She and her friends know their numbers very well, don't they Kenny?" Mr. Grant asked him.

"Yeah, they do," he proudly replied. "I wonder, did you teach her how to play Bingo, Mr. Grant?" he questioned. (B-I-N-G-O and *Bingo* was his name-o)

Laughter always makes the day go faster!

In Mrs. Hansen's 7th grade Art class, the students were asked to learn the terminology of the words "shades" and "values" of color, for a colored pencil butterfly project they were currently working on. She taught them that the value of color refers to the depth of color referring to light, medium, or dark. The shade of color refers to how dark it is. It is the combination of a hue and black. For example, burgundy is a shade of red. Hunter is a shade of green, and rust is a shade of orange.

On a pop quiz at the end of the week, Mrs. Hansen asked the question, "What does it mean when we say the "value" of color?" One amusing answer pertaining to the value of color from Nicholas Dempsey was how much that "color costs." His response was about $7.00 or $8.00. When Mrs. Hansen questioned that answer, Nicholas replied, "Each of the Prismabrand colored pencils I own costs about $1.00, and we are to blend with 6-8 different colored pencils, so that would cost somewhere around $6-$8.

"Good answer Nick, we could adapt that to Mrs. Bobby's math lesson," Mrs. Hansen replied.

5th grade language arts teacher, Mrs. Cortez was teaching her students all about punctuation. She stressed to her class over and over, "Remember class, all punctuation marks always go "inside" the quotation marks." One of her students, Marcus, did just that. Instead of this—"What a great hit!"

His looked like this—"What a great hit'!' (inside the quotation) Ah, maybe just one more time to stress the punctuation rules for Marcus.

Apprehensiveness and doubt, separation anxiety and school rules to learn, come with every kindergarten child at the beginning of a new school year. Usually the new routine settles in after the first few weeks of classes. Most children adapt rather well to the structure, consistency, and positive foundation introduced by their highly qualified and caring kindergarten teachers.

Mrs. Goretski had just completed her second year as a public elementary schoolteacher at Drums Elementary School. A witty charm characterized this vibrant young woman; she had the polish and grace of her childhood dance performances and recitals, and continued as an amateur dance group instructor after her school day ended. Wonderful with all of the children she taught both in and out of school, she retained the attention and trust of her students with her daily teaching.

One kindergarten newcomer, Brianna Jones, came into school each day with her father. Hugs and kisses of farewell in the vestibule were given and then off into the cafeteria she went to sit and wait, until the bell rang for all of the students to be dismissed to their classrooms. To her locker slowly she'd walk, feet dragging, head lowered, to hang her coat and backpack, then carried her folder along with her mid-morning snack into Room A101.

Mrs. Brogan walked the hallway toward the cafeteria each morning at 8:30 A.M., most days greeting Brianna and her father at the doorway. The first six weeks of school were difficult for Brianna to leave her father's side, and she usually began to cry out loud for him in the breakfast room. "I want my daddy," she'd wail. "I wa, wa, want my, my, my Daddy!" Tears and quivering sobs, puffy pink eyes, fists rubbing at her eyes and nose, there she stood as a composite picture of sad-eyed Eeyore from Winnie the Pooh, with the "Oh Bother" attitude, she began each day. Mrs. Brogan was cued from Mrs. Goretski, that greater attention given to Brianna when she cried, brought the tears on even heavier. Within a few weeks, Mrs. Brogan agreed to a hug when she was dry-eyed and ready to go off to her classroom.

The start of school and the separation of her father and mother were the causes of little Brianna's distress. Children are deeply affected in numerous ways by any turbulence within their family structure. As an only child, Brianna lived at home with her father. Occasionally, she slept over at her Aunt Betty's apartment house, and Mrs. Brogan always knew when she did. Aunt Betty and she did creative crafts and coloring pages before she came to school. She'd have a surprise to show off when Aunt Betty brought her in the morning.

The end of October soon approached. Mrs. Brogan began to ask the children how or who they were going to dress up as for Halloween. The annual visit to The Providence Place elderly residential home "in costume" would take the Kindergarten classes on school buses at 9:30A.M., then back to the school for lunch. Then they enjoyed the great classroom Halloween parties in the afternoon. The last Friday of October was an official "No work at school today, Party Day!"

Taylor, in his soft, deep, raspy voice said, "I'm going to be a fireman."

Chelsea beamed and replied, "I'm going to be a cheerleader!"

"A Hershey Kiss!" shouted Carley and her cousin Hunter said, "An alien from outer space, with supersize ears!"

Brianna tugged on Mrs. Brogan's pant leg, looked up at her and said softly, "I'm going to be a cowgirl. My Daddy said they only know cowgirls at the nursing home."

"A cowgirl!" replied Mrs. Brogan, "I can't wait to see all of you children dressed for Halloween!"

The classrooms and hallways of the school were decorated with glittering pumpkins, black crows hidden inside cornstalks, flying bats and cats, ghoulish ghosts and goblins. A magical feeling whisks a child into a fantasyland of make-up and make-believe on Halloween.

Mrs. Brogan donned her tall black witch's hat, extending her height to 6 ½ feet. She was dressed in orange and black, with matching striped socks and began her walk toward the west wing doorway on Halloween day. As she drew closer, the double doors opened and there before her eyes stood the most adorable little cowgirl that she had ever seen! Brianna's father bent over and kissed his daughter softly on her cheek. She walked timidly toward Mrs. Brogan clasping her talking brown spotted plush pony on a stick. Brianna wore a red velvet vest and matching red skirt with boots trimmed with white satin. Her dirty blonde hair was tied up in ponytails, with a wide brimmed red cowgirl hat on top of her head. The outfit, no doubt, was hand-made by her Aunt Betty. "Oooh, you're a witch!" she said to Mrs. Brogan.

"And you are a very pretty cowgirl," Mrs. Brogan replied.

Into the cafeteria they walked and "oohed" and "awed" at the other kindergarten children all ready for their field trip to Providence Place to visit with the senior citizens who resided there. The kindergarten classes had practiced Halloween songs and anticipated a game of Bingo with the residents.

Close your eyes and visualize a room filled with seventy to ninety-five year-old senior citizens, grandmas and grandpas, great grandmas and grandpas.

Enter two busloads of fifty, five-year-old children dressed in their finest, funniest, cutest, scariest, most original and creative Halloween costumes. What a joy for those loving old-timers to have the pleasure on a brisk autumn day of a welcome visit from these tenderhearted youngsters!

Later that morning when Mrs. Brogan shelved books in the library, she noticed that the twin yellow school district buses had arrived at the front of the building. She walked to the entrance of the school to hold the doors open as the schoolchildren, teachers and parent volunteers exited the buses and re-entered the school. She was able to exclaim her excitement and compliments to them as they passed by her. They returned with smiling faces and a Halloween treat as mementos of their field trip to the nursing home that morning.

Mrs. Brogan waited as Brianna approached her. She exclaimed in excitement, "They knew every one of us! They knew me as a cowgirl and Taylor as a fireman and Shawna as a princess!" She put her arms in the air and said, "They even knew Hunter the Alien too!"

Take time one day out of your busy schedule and make a visit to a local senior citizens center or nursing home. Plan a visit to your nearest elderly housing development or nearby neighbor. Feel their joy with your presence, share a story, laugh a little, remember years past and bring out the inner child in their eyes and hearts, as well as in your own. That special visit will warm your hearts and bring tons of happiness to theirs.

When I substituted as a teacher's aide, many times I was called to work with a handsome, autistic boy named Gerry. I first met Gerry in the Old Drums School on South Old Turnpike Road when he was in 4$^{th}$ grade. Gerry always asked questions. "Did you like John Belushi when he played in the *Blues Brothers*?" or "how about the guy who played Luke in *Star Wars*. Did you think the Austin Powers' movies were funny? What part did you like the best?" If you would allow him, Gerry could ask questions all day long. His daily aide at school, Liz, was Gerry's enabler up until he entered high school and started ninth grade.

I would see him from time to time as we both were members of the same parish in town. I ran into him at the grocery store one day. He was peering into the frozen department looking over and trying to decide which flavor of frozen yogurt to get. "Hi Gerry," I said to him. "How are you?"

"Fine LeAnne, how are you?"

"I am very well, thank you," I replied. "What are you looking for?" I asked him.

"Oh my mom, she wants some kind of low fat yogurt, but I don't know what to get."

"What are you up to now that you're finished with school?" I asked him.

"I'm a cook," he replied.

"Oh, that's great, Gerry. Where?"

"I cook in the kitchen at the URS" (United Rehabilitation Services, a service which provides employment opportunities for adults who live with disabilities in our Greater Hazleton Area.)

"What do you cook?" I asked him.

"Anything they tell me to," he said, "except I can't put too much spices in the chili. They don't like it hot. Does your son like it hot?" he asked me.

"No, but his Uncle Francis does," I told him.

"Does he have a bike?"(motorcycle) he asked.

"No, do you Gerry?"

"Yeah, I have my Dad's. He gave it to me in his last will and testament."

Gerry had lost his dad a few years back at a weekend canoe trip when Gerry was an Eagle Scout. He had suddenly taken a heart attack while out in the canoe on the Delaware River and he was unable to get to the hospital quickly enough. It was a shock to those who knew him.

I asked him, "Do you drive it?"

"Heck no," he said. "I don't even have my license."

"Here comes your Mom, Gerry."

"I still don't know what she wants," he said to me again.

His mother, Helen Anne and I spoke for a few minutes. I said how good it was to see Gerry and that he sounded as though he was doing well at his job.

"Well, Gerry," his mother said, "how about if we look for raspberry walnut and cherry vanilla."

"OK, mom," he said.

We said "Good-Bye." It is always nice to see Gerry and his mom. It's also gratifying to see a special needs child work his way through school and acquire a job that will sustain his basic needs. See you soon, Gerry.

We are now entering into the reputable Dennison Township Middle School hallway, as the 7th graders are led by their teacher Mr. Schadder to the auditorium for a midday assembly about drug and alcohol abuse. Loudly and clearly, Eli Edney farts. After the initial blast, his classmates begin to snicker and laugh. Who wouldn't? And it smells. Bad. Real bad.

Mr. Schadder, a first year teacher thought to himself, "What am I supposed to do? I can't reprimand him. Gas happens." The look he gave Eli was not in disregard of his flatulence, but displeasure because of the continued outburst from the students.

Eli, noticing that all eyes were upon him said to his teacher, "You know what they say, Mr. Schadder, the smeller's the feller!"

After that comment, Mr. Schadder lost his composure and chuckled with the class. Clear the hallways! Open all doors! Fumigate the area! (And Eli, if at all possible, put the next one on hold!)

It was early September, the 9th I recall, at the familiar old Drums School, and lunch was being served in the cafeteria, which was on the base floor of the building. Mrs. Ervin began to situate her first grade class in order at table #2, next to the kindergarteners. Like leading a herd of horses to water or a marching army of ants, one behind the other headed toward a picnic lunch, kids require consistency and practice learning the rules of the lunchroom.

There's always a snag, one kid who resists following the rules, that square block trying to fit into the round hole. It was the handsome young lad, Logan Lowery, son of fashion designer, Lucinda Lowery, acting out like the bucking bronco. He began to dart in and out of line. He crawled under the table, proceeded to stand up on the bench, and threw his arms in a King Kong thrust over his head. The tone in the lunchroom began to escalate. Mrs. Ervin reached for her handy-dandy silver monogrammed whistle. She blew it until her face turned crimson red, and you could almost see the smoke coming from her ears. "Logan Lowery, FREEZE!" she commanded.

Logan froze, looked Mrs. Ervin square in the eyes and said, "I do not have to listen to you."

"Mother of Mercy!" her eyes widened, her nostrils flared. She was absolutely appalled by the behavior of this first grade boy. Her next words were, "Principal Warner will be notified of your behavior in this lunchroom today, Mr. Lowery! You may sit over here by me and eat your lunch."

Anyone else who remotely had a passing thought of any other mischievous behavior, quickly held his breath and lowered his eyes to avoid Mrs. Ervin's malicious glare. After the lunch bell rang and the children were settled back in their classrooms, an announcement came overhead into Mrs. Ervin's classroom. "You may send Logan Lowery with an escort to the principal's office now." There was no flinching from Master Lowery. He was as stiff as a tree trunk. The teacher said that Tattletale Tanya Evans could escort Lord Logan. He quietly got up out of his chair, waited for Tanya and the hall pass, and processed down the hallway, two doors to the right, into Principal Warner's office.

Little Logan sat in the straight backed wooden chair next to his desk, while Tanya sat with the secretary, Mrs. Gallows, and stared at the mole on her chin. The principal asked if Logan thought his behavior was appropriate in the lunchroom today. He also added that a telephone call would be made to his mother at her office. Logan flittered and fumbled as his mind raced to come up with a good answer for him. "Oh please," he thought to himself, not my mother! She'll ground me for a month, maybe two, and take away my satellite dish and my 42 inch plasma TV!"

When asked about his inappropriate behavior in the lunchroom for the second time, he answered Principal Warner, "I am truly sorry for the way I acted today. I cannot promise that it won't happen again, Mr. Warner. There are these clowns in my head and they told me to do it. I just can't help it."

Davey and Sissy moved from Tuscaloosa, Alabama, to Honey Hole, Pennsylvania, to live with their Grandma and Grandpa on their dairy farm. The Miller's had been a farming family for years in the area and welcomed their grandchildren with wide open arms. Grammy and Grampy Chicken, their grandkids called them. Davey and Sissy didn't have much, but they had Grammy and Grampy Chicken. Back home in Alabama, they were told their Mom and Dad had to get things evened out; things were a little bumpy. They had to wait for smooth sailing again. So, they hopped on a train straight to Honey Hole.

The children started at the Honey Hole Elementary School in late November. Because they emigrated from the south, cold winters with blustery winds and drifting snow were strange new sights for the siblings. Imagine, never having the opportunity to open your mouth wide, stick your tongue out as long as a ruler, and try to have a beautiful snowflake softly land in your mouth! (Honestly, a few flurries from time to time would suit me just fine, forgetting the heavy snowfalls, accumulating ice and Nor'easters.) Davey and Sissy (Elizabeth Ann) thought stars had fallen from the sky.

I remember how "bundled up" they were one blustery, wintry day in January. From a distance, I saw them coming down the hallway, headed toward their classrooms. They looked and walked like two astronauts on the moon, minus the zero gravity factors. Only their watery eyes and running noses were visible. Davey looked up at me and said, "We need help. I can't move my arms to help Sissy and me get out." I stopped the twosome at their lockers, sat them down on the floor and yanked off their boots, began to unravel their scarves and unzip them from their puffy snowsuits.

"It's mighty cold today," Sissy quivered.

"My gloves are warm," Davey chimed in.

Davey was a constant mover like the Energizer Bunny. He was mesmerized by the Power Rangers and Harry Potter. Sissy's sweet voice was non-stop like the second-hand on a clock, and she so loved Tweety and Tinkerbell. Motion and chatter; two new challenges to the Second grade.

Grammy and Grampy Chicken picked them up every day after school, kept them home when they were sick, came to conferences with their teachers, and always had enough lunch money in their lunch accounts. A wealth of love surrounded them. Adjusted, they had become. February, March and April blew by in that school year. In mid-May, as the school year wound down to the last few weeks, the call came from Alabama that smooth sailing had arrived. The time had come for Davey and Sissy to go back home. On the first of June, Grammy and Grampy Chicken boarded the train with Sissy and Davey, for the departing ride to Alabama. "Good-bye, Davey. Farewell, Sissy." We shall miss those two special kids at Honey Hole Elementary.

Mr. Garvey, Social Service Director and Counselor, shared a personal story, early one Thursday morning in December with me. He said sadly, "My mother never read to me as a child. I attended summer programs in my hometown to learn how to read. It gives me piece of mind when I listen to you read to the children in the library." A valuable lesson learned, indeed. Read to your kids; in turn they will grow with a yearning, eager heart and mind. They in turn, will become readers and read to their own children.

Sometimes you have an unusually bad day. One morning Miss Kozel, one of our kindergarten teachers, started her day by having a wild turkey fly into her windshield on her way to school. The bird smashed her windshield; she had to call Mr. Davis, the principal, to get coverage for her class until she made it into school, have her vehicle towed to a garage, and find a ride to school. Yet, there is someone else to think about. When IEP's (Individualized Education Program) and report card grades are due, St. Patrick's Day and Easter fall within the same week, and when you just get your class settled after gym class, and there happens to be a fire drill, there is someone to think about. When you're down with the flu, are disgusted with the price of oil and gasoline, and grocery prices are on the rise, your class is getting another new student, it rains for six days straight, or the clouds deliver 16" of snow, think about how lucky you are to be here today. Lucky to see the sun rise, to smell the fresh air, to see the sunset, to hold your kids and hug your dog, to be blessed to have a family and a few friends. Thank God for the little things in your life.

I think of a young boy who came into the library one day with his mother and our guidance counselor and our principal. His name was Mark, and he would be attending kindergarten next fall. He was having a tour of our school. With God's grace and goodness, we shall see him in the fall.

Mark was holding an oversized rectangular piece of cardboard in his hands. It was yellow on the side facing me, white with writing on the side he held towards himself. I spoke with him and welcomed him and asked Mark if he could show me what was on the white side. "It's a big check," he said, "made out to me."

The amount read $1,018.00. This amount came from a fundraiser that the school had by placing empty coffee cans in each classroom for teachers and students to donate change for Mark. The money raised would be put toward young Mark's medical bills. Mark has a rare type of cancer and had undergone hours of surgery and countless radiation and chemotherapy treatments. He stood proudly in the entrance of the library holding his check. He seemed timid, thin, and pale, and he had lost his hair obviously from the treatments.

When my life from day to day becomes hectic, disrupted or turbulent, stressful, sorrowful, I think of little Mark. I pray for what God has given me and pray that God might bring a little miracle to little Mark. Say a prayer for him too.

"Remember", Mrs. Mason reminded her 3$^{rd}$ grade class every day to regain their attention, "you are twenty-four well-behaved, intelligent people."

Christopher looked up at his kindergarten teacher Mrs. Nesler, on the first day of school and whispered to her, "My mother told me if you are not good in school, you get sent to Jail School. In Jail School," he said softly, "you have to make your own dinner." Chris was also the same boy who got off the school bus one morning with a massive wad of gum in his goldenrod blonde hair. A clump of his hair stood erect like the Pledge of Allegiance on the center of his scalp. He said he didn't know how it got there and it didn't seem to bother him a bit. Mrs. Nesler tried her best to remove it, but thought it best to have his mother cut it out. She didn't think there was any other option. Chris was a sweet boy who liked to tell tall tales. I don't think Chris was a candidate for Jail School. He was just a little like Dennis the Menace.

Miss Marino watched Logan walk into school. He bent down to pick up a scrap of newspaper off the floor to check out what it was. The tattered picture was of a young girl around 11 years old. She had long dark hair and dark eyebrows. She was grinning as if she had won an award for first place in a Spelling Bee. On her face, inked in with blue pen were warts on either side of her mouth, eraser whited out eyes, and there were three triangle shapes along her chin line that resembled a beard. Miss Marino said to Logan, "I bet you never draw on newspaper pictures like this, do you Logan?" as she gazed at the picture with him. "Well, I only do it in my catechism workbook," he replied.

Every Friday, first period, was Ms. Campbell's class scheduled library time with librarian Brogan. Her second grade students were always excited when they had library. Choosing a new book to read each week was so important for them, and it was fun too. They also enjoyed seeing Mrs. Brogan and her library friends, dozens of stuffed animals recycled from her two sons.
Renowned children's authors, such as, Dr. Seuss (Theodor Geisel) Jan Brett, Tomie DePaola, Marc Brown, and Eric Carle, led the kids on adventures about silly rhymes and riddles, families, animals and real life stories. The students asked for certain titles, subjects and characters each week.
Ryan's dimples beamed as he eyed the book titled *ABC Dog*. On the cover was a photograph of a jumping Jack Russell terrier popping out of a clown covered Jack-in-the-box. Sunny yellow stars tossed on a blue sky background

lay behind the dog. Simply enough, the book pictured cleverly dressed-up dogs for every letter of the alphabet. With colorful, comical photographs, it is a sweet picture book for all ages. From Aa for Afghan Angel to Bb for Beagle Baking, each page of pups was a trip to a puppy farm feeling. From the Flying French Bulldog to the Glamorous Golden Retriever, Outstanding Old English Sheepdog, Shepherd Santa, Weimaraner Wedding to Yoga Yorkie, the book positively put a grin on the face of children.

This book was definitely Ryan's choice. He proudly presented his library card to Librarian Brogan. She proceeded to scan his card along with the barcode on the back of his book. "I'll take good care of it until next Friday, the 10th," he told Mrs. Brogan. He quickly walked back to his seat to begin looking at his new library book.

After each student had his or her book checked out, Librarian Brogan invited the children to the reading area in the far corner of the library. She always had one or two special books to read to the children as they gathered around her on the floor. After reading, she would choose one of her library friends to help line the children up at the doorway. With new library books in hand, arms down and lips zipped, the children marched out into the hallway, led by Ms. Campbell.

It was early Wednesday morning that next week before the bell rang to start the school day, when Ryan approached Mrs. Brogan. Head slightly lowered, he mumbled under his breath, "My dog ate my library book." His eyes were wide and his eyebrows arched as he told the story to her. "I looked and looked," he said, and I couldn't find my *ABC Dog* book. It wasn't in my backpack and wasn't in my room," he replied. "I asked my brother if he had taken it," Ryan continued. Ryan's brother Mark said that the last time he had seen the book, it was near Sasha's bed. "Sasha's my dog," he told Mrs. Brogan. "She is not a very big dog. She's a mix. German Shepard, husky and Pomeranian I think."

Librarian Brogan held back a chuckle. His explanation was so precise, serious and honest. She wanted to be certain Ryan was comfortable telling her the story. "Well, I can understand why Sasha was so curious, Ryan," she said. "Sasha was probably looking for a photograph of herself in that *ABC Dog* book. Maybe when she saw her photo was not included, she scratched and chewed at the pages a bit. Not to worry, Ryan, we have another copy of the book in the library."

Ryan's mother insisted upon paying for the damaged book.

"Do you want me to bring the book back?" he asked Mrs. Brogan.

"Oh heavens no," she replied. "You can keep the book and read it to Sasha anytime you like."

And I thought dogs only ate homework!

Michael Pertschuk is in 5th grade, Mr. Jenkins' homeroom. I knew Michael was a special needs child and had a disability; however, I was unaware of what disability he acquired until I spoke with his mom, Eileen, at the Spring Book Fair. She shared a very touching story with me that day. We were talking about books, naturally, and she said that Michael had misplaced his library book, *Astronomy*. "With Michael and his autism," she said, "he normally takes a non-fiction book out of the library." Fiction books, telling an imaginative story, were difficult for him to retain or find the meaning of. His mind could not process that type of reading material very well. I told her not to worry; it was probably in his classroom or his locker.

Eileen began to tell me that she was training to compete in a triathlon coming up in August. She swam 100 laps that very morning, and said she had hours of training to do in order to get her body in shape for the competition. Her goal was not about winning the race; her goal was to finish the race for her own self-satisfaction. A triathlon is an athletic contest that is a long distance race consisting of three phases; swimming, bicycling, and running. I admired her dedication to such a strenuous sport. She told me that exercise was the one thing she did for herself. With Michael and his sister Madison, her husband, house, pets and numerous volunteer activities, exercise was her outlet.

On Saturday, April 12$^{th,}$ at the Lehigh Parkway in Allentown, Pennsylvania, more than 7,000 people came together to walk a 3.2 mile trail for autism research and to raise awareness about the increasing prevalence of autism. She and Michael had participated in the event nationally sponsored by Toys "R" Us. The organization, called Autism Speaks, Walk Now for Autism, has numerous programs throughout the United States. The walk was to raise funds for awareness of children with autism and raised $462,000. "It was a phenomenal experience," Eileen told me, giving another part of herself to help her son. What touched her heart the most was what Michael asked her when they were approaching the finish line.

"Mom" Michael said to her, "does this mean that when we finish walking, I'll be cured?"

Her eyes filled up as she relived the moment with me. She cried when Michael asked her this, and said to him, "No Mike, it won't, but you know you are going to be just the perfect kid you are right now."

She went on to tell me that Michael calls his autism *Jumble Brain*, because that is how he feels, Eileen said.

"When I grow up," he said to his mother, "I want to be a scientist that cures jumble brain. I don't want any kids to have this or feel like this, or to get picked on like I do. That's what I wanna do, Mama." I am very proud and honored to know this special family.

Mrs. Heller drove her son Robbie to school every day and arrived at approximately 8:35A.M. She'd walk Robbie in through the main entrance and stop in the lobby. Before her departure, they chatted, and then they would whisper softly to one another.

"I'll miss you," Robbie would say.

"I'll miss you more," his mother would reply.

"I love you,"

"I love you too, baby," she'd say to him.

"See you at 3:20."

"See you at 3:20."

"Don't be late."

"Won't be late."

"I'll wait for you over by the first window, OK, Mom?"

"I'll meet you," his mother would say.

"Oh and Mom, don't forget to tell Chloe (the brand new lab pup who already chewed a hole in his Spongebob hat) to be a good girl today."

"I won't forget," she'd reply.

After the morning chitchat, came the morning pep routine. With arms and hands extended, knees slightly bent and bobbling, in unison they'd clap their hands three times, and blow each other a kiss. Then Robbie would reluctantly turn and walk away, oftentimes turning back toward his mother for one last important matter to discuss. With tissue in hand, he'd enter the cafeteria, where the children waited for the bell to ring. He would always turn and give me a smile and walk over to the very first window to catch a glimpse of his mother returning to their car.

One day, after the Christmas holiday break, Rob was feeling very, very lonely. After he waved to his mother by the first window, he sat down by the first cafeteria table facing the windows. The tears began to roll down his cheeks. He had his head lowered and looked heartbroken. I was just about to go over to talk with him. I seemed to be a little too late. His first grade classmates wandered over, Wally followed by Evan and Daniel. His friends sat beside him and immediately they began to cheer him up. Soon, Robbie was smiling, and then chuckling. In a snap, the atmosphere was transformed. Guess it's true when they say, "That's what friends are for."

Miss Lia Fischer, a pleasant executive secretary at the Administration Building, shared this story about a young man she had the pleasure of meeting. Last year, one day in late October, I looked up from my desk and saw a young man walking toward me. He wore freshly pressed khaki pants with a green and gold striped polo shirt. I noticed under his muscular arms, two metal crutches that he needed to assist him in getting around. When he reached my desk, he gave me a big smile and said, "My name is Kevin Tancin, and I'm hoping you can help me. I'd love to be involved with one of our sports teams at the high school. I obviously can't play, but I just want to be a participant. I can and will do anything. Please help me get involved."

I tried with my entire power to hold back the tears that filled my eyes for the determination of this young man and decided to make it a mission to get this student connected to a team. He relayed that he was a freshman, and he seemed very intelligent, polite and mannerly. He exuded tons of self-confidence and appeared to be very self-sufficient. He had no one helping him get around or carrying his books. He transported his books in a large denim sack that hung from his neck. I didn't really know this boy, but I was certainly proud of him.

I got the impression that although he had a physical disability, he was not going to let it get him down or deter him from doing anything that he wanted to do. I called the high school's athletic director, Mr. Barry, who instructed me to contact the head varsity basketball coach. I made arrangements for the head coach, Mr. Joseph, to meet with the young man, and, sure enough, Coach made him a part of the basketball team. Kevin was thrilled because he loved basketball and was very knowledgeable of the game. I was so pleased at how this all unfolded. Every now and then we get a wake up call and realize that the things we take for granted in life are very precious to us.

New students arrive and other students depart throughout the school year. Here today, gone tomorrow; adjusting and readjusting; new friends and old friends; the good listener is always there, inside the school, faithfully watching over the kids. Children that touch my heart and touch my soul.

Remember this: The world may end tomorrow, but I'll know that I have done my best for today. "Hey kids, do the best that you can every day." TTFN, Mrs. Brogan

In conclusion: Many names, faces and places I have forgotten over the years. I can honestly share with you the names of the admired and respected teachers that taught me through my Kindergarten through 8th grade school years. My teachers made an impact upon my life. Haven't yours?

| | |
|---|---|
| Kindergarten: | Miss Bitetti |
| Grade 1: | Mrs. Gauze |
| Grade 2: | Miss Lesser |
| Grade 3: | Miss McClellan |
| Grade 4: | Miss Lang |
| Grade 5: | Mr. Scalleat |
| Grade 6: | Mr. Lutz and Mr. Matisak |
| Grade 7: | Mr. Yourechko |
| Grade 8: | Mr. Korol |

## LeAnne Brogan

Attention teachers: Here is a statement for you.

Know that you mold young minds, instill creativity and confidence, and uncover special abilities, talents and gifts within your students. Of course, there are those special few each year that challenge you to the end of your rope. Most importantly remember you do leave a "mark" or a lasting impression on all of the students that you have taught in your classrooms throughout your careers. Many, many thanks to each and every one of you.

Printed in the United States
152600LV00015B/155/P